## STAR TREK 4

Ready to face any danger the solar sphere could thrust at them, they ranged to the outer limits of experience looking for adventure.

**Kirk**—Captain of the **Enterprise**, the top man in Space Service—Starfleet Command—he alone makes the decisions, so grave that they can affect the future course of civilization throughout the Universe.

**Spock**—Science Officer—Inheriting a precise, logical thinking pattern from his father, a native of the planet Vulcan, Mr. Spock maintains a dangerous Earth trait . . . an intense curiosity about things of alien origin.

**McCoy**—"Bones," the magnificent medic, a dour super-Scot and the last word in first aid.

With a crew of 400 skilled specialists, the mammoth space ship **Enterprise** blasts off for intergalactic intrigue in the unexplored realms of outer space.

# STAR TREK 4

### Adapted by
## JAMES BLISH

Based on the exciting
television series created
by GENE RODDENBERRY

· BANTAM BOOKS ·
TORONTO · NEW YORK · LONDON
A NATIONAL GENERAL COMPANY

RLI: VLM 6 (VLR 7-7)
IL 6-up

STAR TREK 4
*A Bantam Book published July 1971*
*2nd printing*
*3rd printing*
*4th printing*
*5th printing*

*Published simultaneously in the United States and Canada*

*Bantam Books are published by Bantam Books, Inc., a National
General company. Its trade-mark, consisting of the words "Bantam
Books" and the portrayal of a bantam, is registered in the United
States Patent Office and in other countries. Marca Registrada.
Bantam Books, Inc., 666 Fifth Avenue, New York, N.Y. 10019.*

PRINTED IN THE UNITED STATES OF AMERICA

To

*DONNA WOODMAN*
and the other new English
STAR TREK fans

# CONTENTS

# PREFACE

As I mentioned in the Preface to STAR TREK THREE, I get a staggering amount of fan mail from the readers of the *STAR TREK* books—far more than I can possibly answer. I'm still getting more and more. I also get letters asking me to adapt particular stories. I keep a running tally of them, to help me make up the table of contents for the next book.

This time, "The Menagerie," an episode by Gene Roddenberry himself, was high on the list. It won the Hugo award for Best Dramatic Presentation of 1967 at the 25th World Science Fiction Convention in New York. A STAR TREK episode won the year after that, too—Harlan Ellison's "The City on the Edge of Tomorrow," which appeared in STAR TREK TWO. Now, alas, no new episodes of STAR TREK are being produced, so it wasn't in competition for the 1970 awards.

Even though STAR TREK is no longer a network television show, it is as popular as ever. As a syndicated show, it is presently being exhibited on over a hundred stations throughout the United States, and in England, too.

And I'm going on with the books, as almost all your letters have asked me to do. As matters stand now, there will be at least four more of them, all within the next year or so.

JAMES BLISH

Harpsden (Henley)
Oxon, England

# ALL OUR YESTERDAYS

## (Jean Lisette Aroeste)

The star Beta Niobe, the computer reported, was going to go nova in approximately three and a half hours from now. Its only satellite, Sarpeidon, was a Class M world which at last report had been inhabited by a humanoid species, civilized, but incapable of space flight. Nevertheless, the sensors of the *Enterprise* showed that no intelligent life remained on the planet.

But they did show that a large power generator was still functioning down there. That meant, possibly, that there were still some few survivors after all, in which case they had to be located and taken off before the planet was destroyed.

Homing the Transporter on the power signal, Kirk, Spock and McCoy materialized in the center of a fairly large room, subdivided by shelving and storage cabinets into several areas. One alcove contained a consultation desk, with shelves of books behind it. Another held several elaborate machines which were obviously in operation, humming and spinning and blinking. Kirk stared at these with bafflement, and then turned to Spock, who scanned them with his tricorder and raised his hands in a slight gesture.

"The power pulse source, obviously," the First Officer said. "But what it all *does* is another question."

Along one side was a less puzzling installation: an audiovisual facility containing several carrels (individual study desks) with headsets, projectors and small screens. The nearby wall was pierced by a door and a window. A tape storage area at the end of the room had been caged in, but its door stood ajar.

1

"May I help you?"

The three officers spun around. Facing them was a dignified, almost imposing man of early middle age. "I am the librarian," he added cordially.

Spock said, "Perhaps you can, Mr. . . . ?"

"Mr. Atoz. I confess that I am a little surprised to see you; I had thought that everyone had long since gone. But the surprise is a pleasant one. After all, a library serves no purpose unless someone is using it."

"You say that everyone has gone," Kirk said. "Where?"

"It depended upon the individual, of course. If you wish to trace a specific person, I'm sorry, but that information is confidential."

"No, no particular person," McCoy said. "Just—in general—where did they go?"

"Ah, you find it difficult to choose, is that it? Yes, a wide range of alternatives is a mixed blessing, but perhaps I can help. Would you come this way, please?" With a little bow, Atoz invited them to precede him to the audio-visual area. Apparently, Kirk thought, Atoz thought the three officers were natives, and that they wanted to go where the others had gone. Well, what better way to find out?

It was impossible not to be surprised, however, when Atoz, whom he would have sworn had been behind them, emerged smiling from the tape storage cage.

"How the devil did he get over there?" McCoy said in a penetrating stage whisper.

"Each viewing station in this facility is independently operated," Atoz said, as if that explained everything. "You may select from more than twenty thousand Verisim tapes, several hundred of which have only recently been added to the collection. I'm sure that you will find something here that pleases you." He turned toward Kirk. "You, sir, what is your particular field of interest?"

"How about recent history?" Kirk suggested.

"Really? That is too bad. We have so little on recent history; there was no demand for it."

"It doesn't have to be extensive," Kirk said. "Just the answers to a few questions."

"Ah, of course. In that case, Reference Service is available in the second alcove to your right."

It was not quite so surprising, this time, to find the incredible Mr. Atoz already waiting for them at the reference desk. But there was something else: Kirk had the instant impression that Atoz had somehow never seen them before; a guess which was promptly confirmed by the man's first words.

"You're very late," he said angrily. "Where have you been?"

"We came as soon as we knew what was happening."

"It is my fault, sir," Spock said. "I must have miscalculated. Remember, the ship's sensors indicated there was no one here at all."

"In a very few hours, you would have been absolutely correct," Atoz said. "You three would have perished— vaporized. You arrived just in time."

"Then you know what's going to happen?" McCoy queried.

"You idiot! Of course I know. Everyone was warned of the coming nova long ago. They followed instructions and are now safe. And you had better do the same."

"Did you say they were *safe?*" asked Kirk.

"Absolutely," Atoz said with pride. "Every single one."

"Safe where? Where did they go?"

"Wherever they wanted to go, of course. It is strictly up to the individual's choice."

"And did you alone send all the people of this planet to safety?"

"Yes," Atoz said. "I am proud to say I did. Of course, I had to delegate the simple tasks to my replicas; but the responsibility was mine alone."

"I believe we've met two of them," Kirk said, a little grimly. "You're the real thing, I take it."

"Of course."

McCoy was already scanning Atoz with his tricorder. "As a matter of fact, he is quite real, Jim. And that may explain the report of the ship's sensors; just one remaining man is a difficult object for detection. Sir, are you aware that you will die if you remain here?"

"Of course, but I plan to join my wife and family when

3

the time comes. Do not be concerned about me. Think of yourselves."

Kirk sighed. The man was single-minded almost to the point of mania. But then, that was just the kind of man who'd be given a job like this. Or the kind of man such a job would soon make him. "All right," he said resignedly. "How? What shall we do?"

"The history of the planet is available in every detail," Atoz said, rising and leading them toward the tape carrels. "Just choose what interests you the most—the century, the date, the moment. But, remember, you are very late."

Kirk and McCoy donned headsets, and Atoz selected tapes from the shelves, inserting one in each viewer.

"Thank you, sir," Kirk said. "We will be as quick as we can." He offered a headset to Spock, but the First Officer shook his head and walked off toward the big machine that had mystified him earlier, and which Atoz now appeared to be activating. At the same time, Kirk's screen lighted and he found himself looking at an empty street—it was little more than an alley—which on Earth he would have guessed to be seventeenth-century English. A quick glance to his left revealed that McCoy's screen showed something even less interesting: an Arctic waste. Atoz certainly had peculiar ideas of . . .

A woman screamed, piercingly.

Kirk jumped to his feet, tearing off the headset. The scream came again—not from the headset, obviously, but from the entrance to the observatory-library.

"Help! They're murdering me!"

"Spock! Bones!" Kirk shouted, charging for the door. "Over here, quick!"

Behind him, Atoz' voice cried out: "Stop! I have not prepared you! Wait, you must be . . ."

As Kirk shot out the door, the voice was cut off as if someone had thrown a switch . . .

. . . and he skidded to a halt in the alley he had seen on the screen!

There was no time for puzzlement. The alley was chill and misty, but real enough and the screams came from

4

around the next corner, followed this time by a man's voice.

"Be sweet, love, and I might have a mind to be generous."

Kirk rounded the corner cautiously. A young man wearing velvet, lace and a sword was struggling with a woman dressed like a gypsy. She seemed to be giving him little trouble; though she was kicking and scratching, his handling was as much amorous as it was brutal. A second, even more foppish young man was lounging against the nearby wall, watching with amusement. Then the woman managed to bite the first one on the hand.

"Ow! Vixen!" He aimed a savage cuff at her cheek. The blow never fell; Kirk's hand closed around his upraised arm.

"Let her go," Kirk said.

The woman wiggled free, and the fop's face hardened. "Come when you are bidden, slave," he said, and aimed a roundhouse blow at Kirk's head. Kirk checked the swing and followed through, and a moment later his opponent was sprawling in the dirt.

The second fop shoved the woman aside and moved threateningly toward Kirk, his hand hovering over his rapier hilt. "You need a lesson in how to use your betters," he said. "Who's your master, fellow?"

"I am a freeman."

This seemed to put the fop almost into good humor again. He smiled nastily and drew his rapier.

"Freedom dresses you in poor livery, like a mountebank—and you want better manners, too, freeman." The rapier point slashed Kirk's sleeve.

"The other's behind you, friend!" the woman's voice called, but too late; Kirk was seized from behind. He elbowed his captor in the midriff and, when he broke away, he had the man's sword in his left hand. These creatures really seemed to know nothing at all about unarmed combat, but it would be as well to put an end to this right now. He drew his phaser and fired point-blank.

It didn't go off.

Dropping it, Kirk shifted sword hands and closed on the second fop. He was only fair as a swordsman, too; his

5

lunges were clumsy enough to allow Kirk plenty of freedom to keep the weaponless first fop on the ropes with left-handed karate chops. The swordsman's eyes bulged when his companion went down for the third time and began to back away.

"Sladykins! He's a devil! I'll have no more of this."

He disengaged and ran, his friend not far behind. Kirk picked up and holstered the ineffective phaser and turned to the woman, who was patting her hair and checking her clothes for damage. The clothes were none too clean, and neither was she, although she was pretty enough.

"Thankee, man," she said. "I thought to be limbered sure when the gull caught me drawing his boung."

"I don't follow you. Are you all right?"

The woman looked him over calculatingly. "Ah, I took you for an angler, but you're none of us. Well, you're a bully fine cope for all that. What a handsome dish you served them, the coxcombs!"

She seemed to be becoming more incomprehensible by the minute. "I'm afraid you may be hurt," Kirk said. "You'd better come back into the library with me. You'll be safe there, and Dr. McCoy can see to those bruises."

"I'm game, luv. Lead and I'll follow. Where's library?"

"Just back there . . ."

But when they got to the alley wall, it was blank. The door through which Kirk had come had vanished.

He prowled back and forth, then turned to the woman, who said, puzzled, "What's wi' you, man? Let's make off before coxcombs come wi' shoulder-clappers."

"Do you happen to remember when you first saw me? Do you remember whether I came through some kind of door?"

"I think that rum gull knocked you in the head. Come, luv. I know a leech who'll ask no questions."

"Wait. It must be here somewhere. Bones! Spock!"

"Here, Captain," the First Officer's voice said at once, to the woman's obvious alarm. "We hear you, but we cannot see you. Are you all right?"

"We followed you," McCoy's voice added, "but you'd disappeared."

"We must have missed each other in the fog."

6

"Fog, Captain?" Spock's voice said. "We have encountered no fog."

"Mercy on us," said the woman. "It's a spirit!"

"No, don't be frightened," Kirk said hastily. "These are friends of mine. They're—on the other side of the wall. Spock! Are you still in the library?"

"Indeed not," Spock's voice said. "We are in a wilderness of arctic characteristics . . ."

"He means that it's cold," McCoy's voice broke in drily.

"Approximately minus twenty-five centigrade. There is no library that we can see. We are at the foot of an ice cliff, and apparently we came *through* the cliff, since there is no visible aperture."

"There's no sign of a door here either," Kirk said. "Only the wall. It's foggy here, and I can smell the ocean."

"Yes. That is the period you were looking at in the viewer. Dr. McCoy, on the other hand, was watching a tape of Sarpeidon's last ice age—and here he is, and I with him because we left the library at the same instant."

"Which explains the disappearance of the inhabitants," Kirk concluded. "We certainly underestimated Mr. Atoz."

The woman, clearly terrified by the disembodied voices, was edging away from him. Well, that wasn't important now.

"Yes," Spock was saying. "Apparently they have all escaped from the destruction of their world by retreating into the past."

"Well, we know how we got here. Can we get back? The portal's invisible, but we can still hear each other. There must be a portion of this wall that only *looks* solid . . ."

He was interrupted by still another scream from the woman, with whom he was beginning to feel definitely annoyed. He turned to find that her attempt to run out of the alley had been blocked by the two fops, who had returned with a pair of obvious constables.

"My friends are back—a couple of, uh, coxcombs I had a run-in with a little earlier. And they've brought reinforcements."

7

"Keep looking, Jim," McCoy's voice urged. "You *must* be close to the portal. We're looking too."

"There's the mort's accomplice," one of the fops said, pointing at Kirk. "Arrest him."

"We are the law," one of the constables told Kirk, "and do require that you yield to us."

"On what charge?"

"Thievery and purse-cutting."

"Nonsense. I'm no thief."

"Jim," McCoy's voice said. "What's happening?"

"Lord help us, what's that?" exclaimed the other constable.

"It's spirits!" the woman cried.

The second constable crossed his sword and dagger and held them before him gingerly. He looked frightened, but he resumed advancing. "Depart, spirits, and let honest men approach."

Kirk seized his advantage. "Keep talking, Bones," he said, edging away.

"They speak at *his* bidding," one of the fops said excitedly. "Stop his mouth and they'll quiet!"

"You must be close to the portal now," Spock's voice said.

"Just keep talk . . ."

But the other constable had crept around to the other side. A heavy blow exploded against Kirk's head, and that was the end of that.

The landscape was barren, consisting entirely of ice and rocks, over which the wind howled mercilessly. The ruined buildings surrounding the library had vanished, and so had the library itself. There was nothing but the ice cliff and, on the other side, the rocky glacial plain stretching endlessly into the distance.

Spock continued to feel carefully along the cliff, trying not to maintain contact for more than a few seconds each time. Beside him, McCoy shivered and blew on his hands, then chafed his ears and face.

"Jim's gone!" the surgeon said. "Why can't we hear him?"

"I am afraid that Mr. Atoz may have closed the portal;

I doubt that I shall find it now, in any event. We had best move along."

"Jim sounded as if he might be in trouble."

"He doubtless was in trouble, but so are we. We must find shelter, or we will very quickly perish in this cold."

McCoy stumbled. Spock caught him and helped him to a seat on a large boulder, noting that his chin, nose and ears had become whitened and bloodless. The First Officer knew well enough what that meant. He also knew, geologically, where they were; in a terminal moraine, the rock-tumble pushed ahead of itself by an advancing glacier. The chances of finding shelter here were nil. It seemed a curious sort of refuge for a time-traveling people to pick, with so many milder environments available at will.

"Spock," McCoy said. "Leave me here."

"We go together or not at all."

"Don't be a fool. My face and hands are getting frostbitten. I can hardly feel my feet. Alone, you'll have a chance—at least to try to get back to Jim!"

"We stay together," Spock said.

"Stubborn, thickheaded . . ."

His voice faded. Spock looked about grimly. To his astonishment, he saw that they were being watched.

In the near distance was a cryptic figure clad in fur coveralls and a parka, its face concealed by a snow mask out of which two eyes stared intently. After a moment the figure beckoned, unmistakably.

Spock turned to McCoy, to find that he had fallen. He shook the medical officer, but there was no response. Spock put his ear to McCoy's chest; yes, heart still beating, but feebly.

A shadow fell across them both. The figure was standing over them; and again it gestured, *Follow me.*

"My companion is ill."

*Follow me.*

Logic dictated no better course. Slinging McCoy over his shoulder, Spock stood. The weight was not intolerable, though it threw him out of balance. The figure moved off among the rocks. Spock followed.

The way eventually took them underground, as Spock

had already deduced that it would; where else, after all, could there be shelter in this wilderness? There were two rooms—caves, really—and one was a sleeping room, fairly small, windowless of necessity, furnished most simply. Near the door was a rude bed on which Spock placed McCoy.

"Blankets," Spock said.

The figure pointed, then helped him cover the sick man. Spock looked through McCoy's medical pouch, found his tricorder, and began checking. The figure sat at the foot of the bed, watching Spock, still silent, utterly enigmatic.

"He cannot stand your weather. Unfortunately, he is the physician, not I. I'll not risk giving him medication at this point. If he is kept quiet and warm, he may recover naturally." He scrutinized the mysterious watcher. "It is quite agreeably warm in here. Have you a reason for continuing to wear that mask? Is there a taboo that prohibits my seeing your face?"

From behind the mask there came a musical feminine laugh, and then a feminine voice. "I had forgotten I still had these things on."

She took off the mask and parka, but her laughter died as she inspected Spock more closely. "Who are you?"

"I am called Spock."

"Even your name is strange. Forgive me—you are so unlike anyone I have ever seen."

"That is not surprising. Please do not be alarmed."

"Why are you here?" the woman asked hesitantly. "Are you prisoners too?"

"Prisoners?"

"This is one of the places—or rather, times—Zor Khan sends people when he wishes them to disappear. Didn't you come back through the time-portal?"

"Yes, but not as prisoners. We were sent here by mistake; or such is my hypothesis."

She considered this. "The Atavachron is far away," she said at last, "but I think you come from somewhere farther than that."

"That is true," Spock said. He looked at her more closely. This face out of the past, eager yet reposeful,

10

without trace of artifice, was—could it be what Earthmen called *touching?* "Yes—I am not from the world you know at all. My home is a planet many light-years away."

"How wonderful! I've always loved the books about such possibilities." Her expression, though, darkened suddenly. "But they're only stories. This isn't real. I'm imagining all this. I'm going mad. I always thought I would."

As she shrank from him, Spock reached out and took her hand. "I am firmly convinced that I do in fact exist. I am substantial. You are not imagining this."

"I've been alone here for so long, longer than I want to remember," she said, with a weak smile. She was beginning to relax again. "When I saw you out there, I couldn't believe it."

Spock was beginning to feel something very like compassion for her, which was so unusual that it confused him—which was more unusual still. He turned back to McCoy and checked the unconscious man with the tricorder; this added alarm to the complex.

"I was wrong not to give him the coradrenaline," he said, taking the hypo out of the medical pouch and using it.

"What's happening? Is he dying? I have a few medicines . . ."

"Contra-indicated. Your physiology may be radically different. But I may have given him too much. Well, it's done now."

The woman watched him. "You seem so very calm," she said, "but I sense that he is someone close to you."

"We have gotten used to each other over the years. Aha . . ."

McCoy groaned, stirred and his breathing harshened, as though he were fighting for air. Spock leaned over him.

"Dr. Leonard McCoy, wake up," he said formally but urgently. Then, *"Bones!"*

McCoy's breathing quieted gradually and Spock stepped back. The surgeon's eyes opened, and slowly came to focus on the woman.

"Who are you?" he asked fuzzily.

"My name is Zarabeth."

Somehow, Spock had never thought to ask that.

11

"Where's Spock?"

"I'm here, Doctor."

"Are we back in the library?"

"We are still in the ice age," Spock said. "But safe, for the moment."

McCoy tried to sit up, though it was obvious that he was still groggy. "Jim! Where's Jim? We've got to find Jim!"

"You are in no condition to get up. Rest now, and I will attempt to find the Captain."

McCoy allowed Spock to settle him back in bed. "Find him, Spock. Don't worry about me. Find him!"

He closed his eyes, and after a moment, Spock nodded silently toward the door. Zarabeth led the way back into the underground living room, then asked, "Who is this Jim?"

"Our Commanding Officer. Our friend."

"I saw only the two of you. I did not know that there was another."

"There—is not. He did not come with us. The time-portal sent him to another historical period, much later than this one. If I am to find him, there is only one avenue. Will you show me where the time-portal is?"

"But your friend—in the other room," Zarabeth said. "He is ill."

"It is true that if I leave him, there is the danger that he may never regain the ship." Spock thought it over. It proved to be peculiarly difficult. "He would then be marooned in this time-period. But he is no longer in danger of death, so my primary duty to him has been discharged . . . If I remain here, no one of our party can aid Captain Kirk . . ."

"You make it sound like an equation."

"It should be an equation," Spock said, frowning. "I should be able to resolve the problem logically. My impulse is to try to find the Captain, and yet—" he found that he was pacing, although it didn't seem to help much. "I have already made one error of judgment that nearly cost McCoy's life. I must not make another now. Perhaps it has to do with the Atavachron. If I knew more about how it works . . . Zarabeth, you say that you are a prisoner here. May I ask . . ."

". . . why? My crime was in choosing my kinsmen unwisely. Two of them were involved in a conspiracy to kill Zor Khan. It wasn't enough to execute my kinsmen. Zor Khan determined to destroy our entire family. He used the Atavachron to send us to places where no one could ever find us."

"Ah. Then the solution is simple. Zor Khan exists no more. You and I can carry McCoy back to the library. I'll send you and McCoy to the ship, and have Mr. Atoz send me to wherever Jim . . ."

"No!" Zarabeth cried, in obvious terror. "I can't go back through the portal now! I will be dead!"

"You cannot go back?"

"None of us can go back," she said, a little more calmly. "When we come through the portal, we are changed by the Atavachron. That is its function. Our basic metabolic structure is adjusted to the time we enter. You can't go back; if you pass through the portal again, you will be dead when you reach the other side."

And there it was. He and McCoy were trapped here, for the rest of their lives. And so was Jim, wherever *he* was.

When Kirk came to, he found himself all too obviously in jail, and a pretty primitive jail at that, lying on a rough pallet which squeaked of straw. Fingering his head and wincing, he got up and went to the barred door. There was nothing to be seen but a gloomy corridor and the cell opposite his. The gypsy was in it.

She seemed to be about to speak to him, but at that moment there were voices in the near distance and, instead, she shrank into a far corner of her cell. In another moment the constable hove into view, leading a man whose demeanor was all too obviously that of a public prosecutor.

"That's the man," the constable said, pointing to Kirk. "That's the mort's henchman."

He let the prosecutor into the cell. The man regarded Kirk curiously. "You are the thief who talks to spirits?"

"Your honor. I am a stranger here."

"Where are you from?"

Kirk hesitated. "An island."

"What is this island?"

"We call it Earth."

"I know of no island Earth. No matter. Continue."

"I'd never seen the lady across the way before tonight when I heard her scream. As far as I could tell, she was being attacked."

"Then you deny that you're the wench's accomplice?"

"Yes. I was reading in the library when I heard her scream." The prosecutor started visibly at the word "library," and Kirk pursued the advantage, whatever it might be. "Perhaps you remember where the library is?"

"Well, well, perhaps your part in this is innocent," the prosecutor said, with some agitation. "I believe you to be an honest man."

"He's a witch!" screamed the woman from her cell.

"Now, wait a minute . . ."

"Take care, woman," the prosecutor said heavily. "I am convinced you're guilty. Do not compound it with false accusation."

"He speaks to unclean spirits! He's a witch. Constable, you heard the voices!"

"It's truth, my lord," the constable said. "I heard the spirit call him. He answered and did call it 'Bones.' "

"He's a witch," the woman insisted. "He cast a spell and made me steal against my wish."

Aghast, Kirk looked into each face in turn. There was no doubt about it; they believed in witches, all of them. The prosecutor, looking even graver than before, asked the constable, with some reluctance, "You heard these— spirits?"

"Aye, my lord. I'll witness to it."

"The 'voices' they heard were only friends of mine," Kirk said desperately. "They were still on the other side of the wall, in the library, my lord."

"I know nothing of this," the prosecutor said agitatedly. "*I* cannot judge so grave a matter. Let someone learned in witchcraft examine him. I will have no more to do with this."

14

"Look, sir. Couldn't you at least arrange for me to see Mr. Atoz? You do remember Mr. Atoz, don't you?"

"I know of no Atoz. I know nothing of this, nothing of these matters. Take him. I will not hear him."

The constable let the prosecutor out, and together they hurried down the corridor.

Kirk called after them, "Only let me speak to you, my lord!"

They vanished without looking back. Kirk shook the bars, frustrated, angry, hopelessly aware that he was alone and friendless here. Across the corridor, the woman's face was contorted with fear and hatred.

"Witch! Witch!" she shrilled. "They'll burn you!"

They took her away later the next day. Kirk scarcely noticed. He was trying to work out a course of action. He had never seen a jail that looked easier to break, but all attempts to think beyond that point were impeded by a growing headache; and when he got up from the pallet to make sure his hands would fit freely through the bars, he had a sudden spell of faintness. Had he caught some kind of bug?

Down the corridor there was a jingling of keys. The jailer was coming with food. It was now or never.

He was sitting on the pallet again when the jailer arrived; but when the jailer straightened from setting down the bowl of food, Kirk's arm was around his throat, his other hand lifting the ring of keys from his belt. Opening the door from the outside, Kirk pulled the terrified man into the cell and shut the door again.

Releasing his grip, Kirk allowed the jailer a single cry, then knocked him out with a quick chop and rolled him under the pallet. End of Standard Escape Maneuver One. With any luck, that cry should bring the constable, and safe-conduct. Curious how dizzy he felt. On an impulse, he lay down and closed his eyes.

He heard hurrying feet, then the creak of the hinges as the newcomer tried the door. The subsequent muffled exclamation told him that he had been luckier than he knew; the man outside was the prosecutor. Kirk emitted a muffled groan.

Shuffling noises, and then the sound of breathing told

him that the prosecutor was bending over him. A quick glance through half-closed lids told him where the nearest wrist was. He grabbed it.

"If you yell, I'll kill you," he whispered with fierce intensity.

The prosecutor neither yelled nor struggled. He merely said, "It will go harder with you if you persist."

"I am being falsely accused. You know it."

"You are to come with me to the Inquisitional Tribunal. There the matter of your witchcraft will be decided."

"There are no such things as witches."

"I shan't say you said so," the prosecutor said. "That is heresy. If they hear you, they will burn you for such beliefs."

"You are the only one who can hear me. Before the Inquisitor, it will be different. I'll denounce you as a man who came from the future, just as I did. Therefore, you too are a witch."

"They would surely burn me as well," the prosecutor agreed. "But what good would that do you?"

"Use your head, man," Kirk said. "I need your help."

"How can I help you? I will do my utmost to plead your innocence. I may be able to get you off—providing you say nothing of the comrades you left behind."

"Not good enough. I want you to help me to return to the library."

"You cannot go back."

"I tell you, I must. My comrades are lost in another time-period. I have to find them. Why don't you go back too?"

"We can never go back," the prosecutor said. "We must live out our lives here in the past. The Atavachron has prepared our cell structure and brain pattern to make life here natural. To return to the future would mean instant death."

"Prepared?" Kirk said. "I am here by accident. Your Mr. Atoz did not prepare me in any way." As he spoke, his temples began to throb again.

"Then you must get back at once. If you were not

16

transformed, you cannot survive more than a few days here."

"Then you'll show me where the portal is?"

"Yes—approximately. But you must find the exact spot yourself. You understand I dare not wait with you . . ."

"Of course. Let's go."

Five minutes later, Kirk was back in the library. It looked as empty as it had when he had first seen it. He checked the contemporary time with the *Enterprise,* shunting aside a barrage of frantic questions. It was seventeen minutes to nova. Evidently, no matter how much time he spent in the past, the gate at its present setting would always return him to this day. It had to; for the gate, there would be no tomorrow.

He drew his phaser. It had not worked in the past, but he was quite certain it would work here. And this time, Mr. Atoz, he thought grimly, you are going to be *helpful.*

McCoy was still abed, but he was feeling distinctly better, as his appetite proved. Zarabeth, who had adopted a flowing gown which made her look positively beautiful, was out in her work area, making something she had promised would be a delicacy.

"I hope the *Enterprise* got away in time," McCoy said.

"I hope it will get away. The event is a hundred thousand years in the future."

"Yes, I know. I wonder where Jim is?"

"Who knows?" Spock said. "We can only hope he is well, wherever he is."

"What do you mean, we can only hope? Haven't you done anything about it?"

"What was there to do?"

"Locate the portal," McCoy said impatiently. "We certainly didn't come very far from it."

"We've been through all that already, Doctor. What's the point of rehashing the subject? We can't get back. Wasn't that clear to you?"

"Perfectly. I just don't believe it. I refuse to give up trying."

"It would be suicide if you succeeded."

17

McCoy sighed. "I never thought I'd see it. But I understand. You want to stay here. I might say, you are highly motivated to remain in this forsaken waste."

And not ten minutes ago, Spock thought, it had been McCoy who had been praising Zarabeth's cooking, and offering other small gallantries. "The prospect seemed quite attractive to you a few moments ago."

"Listen to me," McCoy said, "you point-eared Vulcan . . ."

Before Spock fully realized what he was doing, he found himself leaning forward and lifting McCoy off the bed.

"I don't like that," he said. "I don't believe I ever did. Now I'm sure."

McCoy did not look in the least alarmed. He simply seemed to by studying Spock intently. "What is it, Spock?" he asked. "What's happening?"

Spock let him drop. "Nothing that shouldn't have happened long ago."

"Long ago," McCoy said softly. The intent scrutiny did not waver. "Yes, I guess so . . . Long ago."

The stare disturbed the First Officer, for reasons he did not understand. Wheeling, he went into the underground living room, where Zarabeth was setting a table. She looked up and smiled.

"Ready soon. Would you like a sample?"

"Thank you, but I am not hungry."

She came over and sat down near him. "I can imagine how you must feel. I know what it's like to be sent here against your will."

"My feelings, as you call them, are of no concern," Spock said. "I have accepted the situation."

"I cannot pretend that I am sorry you are here, though I realize that it is a misfortune for you. I am here against my will, too, just as you are."

"I'm sorry I know of no way to return you to your own time."

"I don't mean that I wish to return," Zarabeth said. "This is my time now. I've had to face that. But it has been lonely here. Do you know what it is like to be alone, really alone?"

"Yes. I know what it is like."

"I believe you do. Won't you eat something? Please?"

"If it pleases you." He walked to the table and surveyed it. He felt a faint shock, but it seemed far away. "This is animal flesh."

There isn't much else to eat here, I'm afraid."

"Naturally, because of the climate. What is the source of heat in this shelter?"

"There is an underground hot spring that furnishes natural steam heat and power."

"And there is sunlight available outside. Excellent. It should be possible to build a greenhouse of sorts. Until then, this will have to do as a source of nourishment." He picked up the most innocuous-looking morsel, surveyed it with distaste, and bit into it. It was quite good; he took another.

"There aren't many luxuries here," Zarabeth said, watching him with evident approval. "Zor Khan left me only what was necessary to survive."

"But he evidently intended you to continue living," Spock said, sampling another dish.

"Yes. He gave me weapons, a shelter, food—everything I needed to live—except companionship. He did not want it said that he had had me killed. But to send me here alone—if that is not death, what is? A very inventive mind, that man."

"But insensitive, to send such a beautiful woman into exile." Instantly, he was badly startled. "Forgive me! I am not usually given to personal remarks."

"How could I possibly take offense?" Zarabeth said.

Spock scarcely heard her. "The cold must have affected me more than I realized. Please—pay no attention. I am not myself."

And that, he thought, was an understatement. He was behaving disgracefully. He had eaten animal flesh—and had enjoyed it! What was wrong with him? He put his hands to his temples.

"I say you are beautiful," he said, feeling a dawning wonder. "But you *are* beautiful. Is it so wrong to tell you so?"

Zarabeth came to him. "I have longed to hear you say it," she said softly.

Then she was in his arms. When the kiss ended, he felt as though a man who had always been locked up inside him had been set free.

"You are beautiful," he said, "beautiful beyond any dream of beauty I have ever had. I shall never stop telling you of it."

"Stay," she whispered. "I shall make you happy."

"My life is here."

*"You lie,"* said a voice from the doorway. Spock spun, furious with McCoy and enjoying it.

"I speak the present truth," he said. "We are here, for good. I have given you the facts."

"The facts as *you* know them. But you are also being dishonest with yourself, and that's also something new for you. You accepted Zarabeth's word because it was what you wanted to believe. But Zarabeth is a woman condemned to a terrible life of loneliness. She will do anything to anybody to change that, won't you, Zarabeth?"

"I told you what I know," Zarabeth said.

"Not quite, I believe. You said *we* can't get back. The truth is that *you* can't get back. Isn't it?"

"She would not jeopardize other lives . . ."

"To save herself from this life alone," McCoy said, "she would lie—and even murder me, the Captain, the whole crew of the *Enterprise,* to keep you here with her." His hand lashed out and caught her by the wrist. "Tell Spock the truth—you would kill to keep him here!"

Zarabeth cried out in terror, and in the next instant Spock found his hands closing around the physician's throat. McCoy did not resist.

"Spock!" he said intensely. "Think! Are you trying to kill me? Is that what you want? What are you feeling? Rage? Jealousy? Have you ever felt them before?"

Spock's hands dropped. His head was whirling. "Impossible," he said. "This is impossible. I am a Vulcan."

"The Vulcan you knew will not exist for another hundred thousand years! Think, Spock—what is it like on your planet now, at this moment?"

20

"My ancestors are barbarians. Irrational, warlike barbarians . . ."

"Who nearly killed themselves off with their passions! And now you are regressing to what they were!"

"I have lost myself," Spock said dully. "I do not know who I am. Zarabeth—can we go back?"

"I do not know. I do not know. It is impossible for me to go back. I thought it was true for you."

"I am going to try, Spock," McCoy said. "My life is there, and I want the life that belongs to me. I must go *now*. There isn't much time—I too am changing. Zarabeth, will you help me find my way to the portal?"

"I—Yes. If I must."

"Let's get dressed, then."

The cold seemed more intense than ever, and McCoy, wrapped in a blanket, still had little resistance to it. He leaned against the ice cliff, partially supported by Zarabeth, who once more was almost anonymous in her furs. Spock tapped the cliff, without success.

"There is no portal here," he said. "It's hopeless, McCoy."

"I suppose you're right."

"You're too ill to stay out here in the cold any longer. Give it up."

And then, faintly, they heard Kirk's voice. "Spock! Can you hear me?"

"It's Jim!" McCoy shouted. "Here we are!"

"Stop, we've found them," Kirk's voice said. "Hold it steady, Atoz. Can you hear me any better?"

"Yes," Spock said. "We hear you perfectly now."

"Follow my voice."

McCoy reached out. His hand disappeared into the cliff. "Here it is! Come on, Spock!"

"Start ahead." He turned to Zarabeth. "I do not wish to part from you."

"I can't come with you. You know that."

"What are you waiting for?" Kirk's voice said. "Hurry! Scotty says we've got to get back on board right now!"

"They will have to come through together," the voice

of Atoz added, "as they went out together. Singly, the portal will reject them."

Spock and Zarabeth looked at each other with despair. He touched her face with his fingertips.

"I did lie," she said. "I knew the truth. I will pay. Goodbye."

Then they were in the library, Kirk pulling them through. Atoz was spinning the dials of the Atavachron frantically, and then, dashing past them, dived into the portal and vanished.

"Atoz!" McCoy called.

"He had his escape planned," Kirk said. "I'm glad he made it." He raised his communicator. "Are you there, Scotty?"

"Aye. It's now or never."

Spock turned toward the portal and raised his fist as if to strike it, but he did not complete the gesture.

"Beam us up. Maximum warp as soon as we are on board."

The library shimmered out of existence, and they were standing in the Transporter Room of the *Enterprise*. McCoy, still wrapped in his blanket, was once more regarding Spock with his intent clinical stare.

"There is no further need for you to observe me, Doctor," Spock said. "As you see, I have returned to the present. In every sense."

"Are you sure? It did happen, Spock."

"Yes, it happened," the First Officer said. "But that was a hundred thousand years ago. They are all dead. Dead and buried long ago."

The ship fled outward. Behind it, the nova began to erupt, in all its terrifying, inhuman glory.

# THE DEVIL IN THE DARK

## (Gene L. Coon)

Janus was an ugly planet, reddish-brown, slowly rotating, with a thick layer of clouds so turbulent that it appeared to be boiling. Not a hospitable place, but a major source of pergium—an energy metal-like plutonium, meta-stable, atomic number 358; the underground colony there was long-established, highly modern, almost completely automated. It had never given any trouble.

"Almost fifty people butchered," Chief Engineer Vanderberg said bitterly. He was standing beside his desk, nervous and urgent; facing him were Kirk, Spock, Lt. Commander Giotto, Doc McCoy and a security officer named Kelly. "Production's at an absolute stop."

"I can see that," Kirk said, gesturing toward the chart on the office wall, which showed a precipitous dip. "But please slow down, Mr. Vanderberg. What's the cause?"

"A monster." Vanderberg stared at the *Enterprise* delegation with belligerent defensiveness, as though daring them to deny it. He was clearly highly overwrought.

"All right," Kirk said. "Let's assume there's a monster. What has it done? When did it start?"

Vanderberg made an obvious effort to control himself. He pushed a button on his desk communicator, which sat near a globe some ten inches in diameter of what appeared to be some dark-gray crystalline solid. "Send Ed Appel in here," he told it, and then added to Kirk, "My production engineer. About three months ago, we opened a new level. It was unusually rich in pergium, platinum, uranium, even gold. The whole planet's a treasure house, but I've never seen anything like this before, even here. We were just setting up to mine it when things began to happen. First the automatic machinery began to disintegrate, piece by piece. The metal just seemed to dissolve away. No mystery about the agent; it was aqua regia, possibly with a little hydrofluoric acid mixed in—vicious stuff. We don't store vast quantities of such stuff here, I can tell you that. Offhand I don't even know what we'd keep it *in*."

"Telfon," Spock suggested.

"Yes, but my point is, we *don't*."

"You said people were butchered," Kirk reminded him gently.

"Yes. First our maintenance engineers. Sent them down into the halls to repair the corroded machinery. We found them—burned to a crisp."

"Not lava, I suppose," Kirk said.

"There is no current volcanic activity on this planet, Captain," Spock said.

"He's right. None. It was that same damn acid mixture. At first the deaths were down deep, but they've been moving up toward our levels. The last man who died, three days ago, was only three levels below this one."

"I'd like to examine his body," McCoy said.

"We kept it for you—what was left. It isn't pretty."

The office door opened to admit a tough-looking, squat, businesslike man of middle age, wearing a number one phaser at his belt.

"You posted guards? Sentries?" Kirk asked.

"Of course. And five of them have died."

"Has anyone seen this—this monster of yours?"

"I did," said the newcomer.

"This is Ed Appel. Describe it, Ed."

"I can't. I only got a glimpse of it. It was big, and kind of shaggy. I shot at it, and I hit it square, too, a good clean shot. It didn't even slow it down."

"Anything a phaser will not affect," Spock said, "has to be an illusion. Any life-form, that is."

"Tell that to Billy Anderson," Appel said grimly. "He never had a chance. I only got away by the skin of my teeth."

"That's the story," Vanderberg said. "Nobody'll go down into the lower levels now, and I don't blame them.

24

If the Federation wants pergium from us, they'll have to do something about it."

"That's what we're here for, Mr. Vanderberg," Kirk said.

"Pretty tough, aren't you?" said Appel. "Starship, phaser banks, energy from anti-matter, the whole bit. Well, you can't get your starship down into the tunnels."

"I don't think we'll need to, Mr. Appel. Mr. Spock, I'll want a complete computer evaluation, with interviews from everyone who knows anything about the events here. Mr. Vanderberg, have you a complete subsurface chart of all drifts, tunnels, galleries and so on?"

"Of course."

Spock had been inspecting the dark-gray sphere on the desk. He stepped forward and touched it. "This, Mr. Vanderberg. What is it?"

"It's a silicon nodule. There's a million of them down there. No commercial value."

"But a geological oddity, to say the least, especially in igneous rocks. Pure silicon?"

"A light oxide layer on the outside, a few trace elements below. Look, we didn't call you here so you could collect rocks."

"Mr. Spock collects information, and it's often useful," Kirk said. "We'll need your complete cooperation."

"You'll get it. Just find this creature, whatever it is. I'm dead sick of losing my men—and I've got a quota to meet, too."

"Your order of priorities," Kirk said, "is the same as mine."

They worked in a room just off Vanderberg's office, feeding data to the *Enterprise's* computer and getting evaluations back by communicator. The charts with which Vanderberg supplied them turned out to be immensely involved—thousands of serpentine lines crossing and recrossing. Their number was incredible, even after allowing for fifty years of tunneling with completely automated equipment. The network extended throughout the entire crust of the planet, and perhaps even deeper.

"Not man-made," Spock agreed. "They may be lava tubes, but if so, they are unique in my experience."

"They won't make hunting any easier," Kirk said. "Bones, what's the word on the autopsy?"

"The plant's physician and the chemists were right, Jim. Schmitter wasn't burned to death. He was flooded or sprayed with that acid mixture."

"Could it eat away machinery, too?"

"Aqua regia will dissolve even gold. What puzzles me is the trace of hydrofluoric acid. It's a very *weak* acid, but there are two things it attacks strongly. One of them is glass—you have to keep it in wax bottles, or, as Spock suggested, telfon."

"And the other thing?"

"Human flesh."

"Hmm. It sounds like a mixture somebody calculated very carefully. Mr. Spock, do you think this monster story could be a blind for some kind of sabotage?"

"Possibly, Captain. For example, Mr. Vanderberg thinks that the creature uses the network of tubes to move through. But if you plot the deaths and the acts of destruction, and their times, you find that the creature cannot possibly have appeared at all these points as rapidly as indicated."

"How recent are those tunnel charts?"

"They were made last year—before the first appearance of the alleged monster, but not long before. Moreover, Captain, a sensor check indicates *no* life under the surface of Janus but the accountable human residents of the colony. We are confronted with two alternatives: either to patrol thousands of miles of tunnels, on foot, in the faint hope of encountering the alleged monster; or to find a plausible human suspect who has managed to manufacture and hide an almost inexhaustible supply of this intractable corrosive, and who has a portable, innocuous-looking carrier for it with a capacity of at least thirty liters."

"I rather prefer the monster theory," McCoy said. "If we catch a man behind these murders, I think we ought to lower him into his own acid vat a quarter of an inch at a time."

"If," Spock said, "is the operative word in either case . . ."

He was interrupted by a distant, heavy boom. The room shuddered, the lights flickered, and then an alarm bell was clanging. A moment later, Vanderberg burst in from his office.

"Something's happened in the main reactor room!" he shouted.

They left at a dead run, Vanderberg leading the way, McCoy bringing up the rear. The trail wound up in a tunnel elaborately posted with signs reading CAUTION: RADIATION—MAIN REACTOR CHAMBER—ONLY AUTHORISED PERSONS BEYOND THIS POINT. The floor of the tunnel looked as though something very heavy had been dragged along it. At the far end was what had once been a large metal door, but which now consisted chiefly of curled strips around a huge hole. Before it was a small, blackened lump which might once have been a man.

Vanderberg recoiled. "Look at that!" Then he hurried toward the ruined door. McCoy knelt quickly beside the charred lump, tricorder out; Kirk and Spock followed Vanderberg.

Inside, the bulk of the reactor was buried in the walls, showing only a large faceplate and a control panel. Pipes crisscrossed the chamber; and an appalled Vanderberg was standing looking down at a sort of nexus of these— a junction that ending in nothing.

Kirk scanned the control panel. "I didn't know anyone still used fission for power."

"I don't suppose anybody does but us. But pergium is money—we ship it all out—and since we have so much uranium nobody wants, we use it here. Or we did until now."

"Explain."

"The main moderator pump's gone. Lucky the cutouts worked, or this whole place would be a flaming mass of sodium."

Spock knelt and inspected the aborted junctions. "Acid again. Like the door. Mr. Vanderberg, do you have a replacement for the missing pump?"

"I doubt it. It was platinum, corrosion-proof, never

27

gave us any trouble; should have lasted forever." Suddenly, visibly, Vanderberg began to panic. "Look, the reactor's shut down now—and it provides heat and electricity and life support for the whole colony! And if we override, we'll have a maximum accident that will poison half the planet!"

"Steady," Kirk said. "Mr. Spock, might we have a replacement on shipboard?"

"No, Captain. To find one, you would need a museum."

Kirk took out his communicator. "Kirk to *Enterprise* ... Lt. Uhura, get me Mr. Scott ... Scotty, this is the Captain. Could you contrive a perfusion pump for a PXK fission reactor?"

"Hoo, Captain, you must be haverin'."

"I'm dead serious; it's vital."

"Well, sir—I could put together some odds and ends. But they wouldn't hold for long."

"How long?"

"Forty-eight hours, maybe, with a bit of luck. It all ought to be platinum, ye see, and I've not got enough, so I'll have to patch in with gold, which won't bear the pressure long ..."

"Get together what you need and beam down here with it."

Kirk put away the communicator and bent upon Vanderberg a look of deep suspicion. "Mr. Vanderberg, I have to tell you that I don't like the way these coincidences are mounting up. How could some hypothetical monster attack precisely the one mechanism in an almost ancient reactor which would create a double crisis like this? And how would it happen to be carrying around with it a mixture of acids precisely calculated to dissolve even platinum—and also human flesh?"

"I don't know," Vanderberg said helplessly. "You suspect sabotage? Impossible. Besides, Ed Appel *saw* the monster."

"He says."

"Ed's been my production chief almost throughout my entire career. I'd trust him with my life. And besides, what would be his motive? Look, dammit, Kirk, my people are being murdered! This is no time for fantasies about spies!

The thing is there, it's free, it's just shut us down right under your nose! Why in God's name don't you *do* something?"

"Captain," Spock's voice said from behind them. "Will you come out and look at this, please?"

Kirk went out into the main tunnel to find the First Officer contemplating a side branch. "This is most curious," he said. "This tunnel is not indicated on any of the charts we were provided. It simply was not there before."

"Too recent to be on the maps, maybe?"

"Yes, but how did it get here, Captain? It shows no signs of having been drilled."

Kirk looked closer. "That's so. And the edges are fused. Could it be a lava tube?"

"That seems most unlikely," Spock said. "Had there been any vulcanism on this level since we arrived, everybody would be aware of it. And it joins a charted tunnel back there about fifty yards."

"Hmm. Let's go back to the ship. I feel the need for a conference."

Spock brought with him into the briefing room of the *Enterprise* one of the strange spherical objects Vanderberg had called silicon nodules, and set it on the table. Then he sat down and stared into it, looking incongruously like a fortune-teller in uniform.

"I think it's mass hysteria," McCoy said.

"Hysteria?" Kirk said. "Dozens of people have been killed."

"Some—natural cause. A phenomenon—and people have dreamed up a mysterious monster to account for it."

Spock stirred. "Surely, Doctor. A natural cause. But not hysteria."

"All right. You asked my opinion. I gave it to you. How do I know? Maybe there is some kind of a monster . . ."

"No creature is monstrous in its own environment, Doctor. And this one appears to be intelligent, as well."

"What makes you think so?"

"The missing pump was not taken by accident," Spock

29

said. "It was the one piece of equipment absolutely essential to the operation of the reactor."

Kirk looked at his First Officer. "You think this creature is trying to drive the colonists off the planet?"

"It seems logical."

"Why just now, Mr. Spock? This production facility was established here fifty years ago."

"I do not know, sir." Spock resumed staring at the round object. "But it is perhaps indicative that Mr. Appel claimed to have hit it with his phaser. He strikes me as a capable but unimaginative man. If he said he hit it, I tend to believe he did. Why was the creature not affected? I have a suggestion, though Dr. McCoy will accuse me of creating fantasies."

"You?" McCoy said. "I doubt it."

"Very well. To begin with, the colonists are equipped only with phaser number one, no need for the more powerful model having been encountered. This instrument, when set to kill, coagulates proteins, which are carbon-based compounds. Suppose this creature's 'organic' compounds are based on silicon instead?"

"Now surely that *is* a fantasy," Kirk said.

"No, it's possible," McCoy said. "Silicon has the same valence as carbon, and a number of simple silicoid 'organics' have been known for a long time. And by the stars, it explains the acids, too. We have hydrochloric acid in our own stomachs, after all. But we're mostly water. Silicon isn't water-soluble, so the aqua regia may be the substrate of the creature's bloodstream. And the hydrofluoric—well, fluorine has an especial affinity for silicon; the result is telfon, which may be what the creature's internal tubing is made of."

"Do you mean to imply," Kirk said slowly, "that this being goes about killing men with its own blood?"

"Not necessarily, Jim It may spit the stuff—and sweat it, too, for all I know. Its tunneling suggests that it does."

"Hmm. It also suggests that it would have to have a form of natural armor plating. But our people have phasers number two, and I defy anything to stand up against that at high power, no matter what it's made of. The question is, how do we locate it?"

30

"I would suggest," Spock said, "that we start at whatever level these silicon nodules were found."

"Why? How do they tie in?"

"Pure speculation, Captain. But it would be helpful if it were confirmed."

"Very well, assemble security forces. I assume that Mr. Scott is already at work on the reactor? Very good, we'll assemble in Vanderberg's office."

"You will each be given a complete chart of all tunnels and diggings under this installation," Kirk told his forces. "You will proceed from level to level, checking out every foot of opening. You will be searching for some variety of creature which apparently is highly resistant to phaser fire, so have your phasers set on maximum. And remember this—fifty people have already been killed. I want no more deaths . . ."

"Except the bloody thing!" Vanderberg exploded.

Kirk nodded. "The creature may or may not attack on sight. However, you must. A great deal depends on getting this installation back into production."

"Mr. Vanderberg," Spock said, "may I ask at which level you discovered the nodules of silicon?"

"The twenty-third. Why?"

"Commander Giotto," Kirk said, "you will take your detail directly to the twenty-third level and start your search from there. Mr. Vanderberg, I want all of your people to stay on the top level. Together. In a safe place."

"I don't know any safe place, Captain. The way this thing comes and goes . . ."

"We'll see what we can do about that. All right, gentlemen. You have your instructions. Let's get at it."

Spock, Kirk, Giotto and two security guards paused on the twenty-third level while Spock adjusted his tricorder. Most of Giotto's men had already fanned out through the tunnels. Kirk pointed to a spot on Giotto's map.

"We are here. You and your guards take this tunnel, which is the only one of this complex that doesn't already have men in it. As you see, they converge up ahead. We'll rendezvous at that point."

31

"Aye aye, sir." The three disappeared into the darkness. Spock continued to scan.

"A strange sensation," the First Officer said. "There are men all about us, and yet because the tricorder is now set for silicon life, it says we are alone down here. No, not quite."

"Traces?"

"A great many—but they are all extremely old. Many thousands of years old. Yet, again, there are many brand new tunnels down here. It does not relate."

"Perhaps it does," Kirk said thoughtfully. "Not tunnels. Not lava tubes. Highways. Roads. Thoroughfares. Mr. Spock, give me an environmental reading, for a thousand yards in any direction."

"Yes, sir—ah. A life-form. Bearing, one hundred eleven degrees, angle of elevation four degrees."

"Not one of our people?"

"No, sir, they would not register."

"Come on!"

They set off quickly, keeping as close on the bearing as the convolutions of the tunnels would allow. Then, ahead, someone screamed—or tried to, for the sound was suddenly cut off. They ran.

A moment later they were looking at a small, blackened lump on the tunnel floor, with a phaser beside it. Grimly, Spock picked up the weapon and checked it.

"One of the guards," he said. "He did not have a chance to fire, Captain."

"And it's only been seconds since we heard him scream . . ."

There was a slithering sound behind them. They whirled together.

In the darkness it was difficult to make out details, except for movement, an undulating crawl forward. The creature was large, low to the ground, somehow worm-like. It was now making another noise, a menacing rattle, like pebbles being shaken in a tin can.

"Look out!" Kirk shouted. "It's charging!"

Both men fired. The monster swung around as the two phaser beams struck its side. With an agonized roar, it leapt backward and vanished.

"After it!"

But the tunnel was empty. It was astonishing that anything of that bulk could move so rapidly. Kirk reached out to touch the wall of the tunnel, then snatched his hand back.

"Mr. Spock! These walls are hot."

"Indeed, Captain. The tricorder says it was cut within the last two minutes."

Kirk heard running footsteps, and then Giotto and a guard, phasers at the ready, appeared behind them.

"Are you all right, Captain? That scream . . ."

"Perfectly, Commander. But one of your men . . ."

"Yes, I saw. Poor Kelly. Did you see the thing, sir?"

"We saw it. In fact, we took a bite out of it."

Spock bent over, then straightened with a large chunk of something in his hand. "And here it is, Captain."

He handed the stuff to Kirk, who examined it closely. Clearly, it was not animal tissue; it looked more like fibrous asbestos. Obviously, Spock's guess had been right.

"Commander Giotto, it looks as though killing this thing will require massed phasers—or a single phaser with much longer contact. Pass the word to your men. And another thing. We already knew it was a killer. Now it's wounded—probably in pain—back in there somewhere. There's nothing more dangerous than a wounded animal. Keep that in mind."

"The creature is moving rapidly through native rock at bearing two hundred one, eleven hundred yards, elevation angle five degrees," Spock said.

"Right." Giotto and the guard went out, and Kirk started to follow them, but Spock remained standing where he was, looking pensive. Kirk said, "What's troubling you, Mr. Spock?"

"Captain, there are literally hundreds of these tunnels in this general area alone. Far too many to be cut by the one creature in an ordinary lifetime."

"We don't know how long it lives."

"No, sir, but its speed of movement indicates a high metabolic rate. That is not compatible with a lifetime much longer than ours."

"Perhaps not," Kirk said. "I fail to see what bearing that has on our problem."

"I mention it, Captain, because if this is the only survivor of a dead race, to kill it would be a crime against science."

"Our concern is the protection of this colony, Mr. Spock. And to get pergium production moving again. This is not a zoological expedition."

"Quite so, Captain. Still . . ."

"Keep your tricorder active. Maintain a constant reading on the creature. We'll try to use the existing tunnels to cut it off. If we have to, we'll use our phasers to cut our own tunnels." Kirk paused, then added more gently, "I'm sorry, Mr. Spock, I'm afraid it must die."

"Sir, if the opportunity arose to capture it instead . . ."

"I will lose no more men, Mr. Spock. The creature will be killed on sight. That's the end of it."

"Very well, sir."

But Kirk was not satisfied. Killing came hard to them all, but Spock in particular was sometimes inclined to hold his fire when his conservation instincts, or his scientific curiosity, were aroused. After a moment, Kirk added, "Mr. Spock, I want you to return to the surface, to assist Mr. Scott in the maintenance of his makeshift circulating pump."

Spock's eyebrows went up. "I beg your pardon, Captain?"

"You heard me. It's vital that we keep that reactor in operation. Your scientific knowledge . . ."

". . . is not needed there. Mr. Scott knows far more about reactors than I do. You are aware of that."

After another pause, Kirk said; "very well. I am in command of the *Enterprise*. You are second in command. This hunt will be dangerous. Either one of us, by himself, is expendable. Both of us are not."

"I will, of course, follow your orders, Captain," Spock said. "But we are dealing with a grave scientific problem right here, so on those grounds, this is where I should be, not with Mr. Scott. Besides, sir, there are approximately one hundred of us engaged in this search, against one creature. The odds against both you and me being killed

34

are—" there was a very slight pause, "two hundred twenty-six point eight to one."

Not for the first time, Kirk found himself outgunned. "Those are good odds. Very well, you may stay. But keep out of trouble, Mr. Spock."

"That is always my intention, Captain."

Kirk's communicator beeped, and he flipped it open. "Kirk here."

"Scotty, Captain. My brilliant improvisation just gave up the ghost. It couldn't take the strain."

"Can you fix it again?"

"Nay, Captain. It's gone for good."

"Very well. Start immediate evacuation of all colonists to the *Enterprise*."

Vanderberg's voice came through. "Not all of them, Captain. Me and some of my key personnel are staying. We'll be down to join you."

"We don't have phasers enough for all of you."

"Then we'll use clubs," Vanderberg's voice said. "But we won't be chased away from here. My people take orders from me, not from you."

Kirk thought fast. "Very well. Get everybody else on board the ship. The fewer people we have breathing the air, the longer the rest of us can hold out. How long is that, Scotty?"

"It's got naught to do with the air, Captain. The reactor will go supercritical in about ten hours. You'll have to find your beastie well before then."

"Right. Feed us constant status reports, Scotty. Mr. Vanderberg, you and your men assemble on level twenty-three, checkpoint Tiger. There you'll team up with *Enterprise* security personnel. They're better armed than you are, so stay in sight of one of them at all times—buddy system. Mr. Spock and I will control all operations by communicator. Understood—and agreed?"

"Both," Vanderberg's voice said grimly. "Suicide is no part of my plans."

"Good. Kirk out . . . Mr. Spock, you seem to have picked up something."

"Yes, Captain. The creature is now quiescent a few thousand yards from here, in that direction."

Kirk took a quick look at his chart. "The map says these two tunnels converge there. Take the left one, Mr. Spock. I'll go to the right."

"Should we separate?"

"Two tunnels," Kirk said. "Two of us. We separate."

"Very well, Captain," Spock said, but his voice was more than a little dubious. But it couldn't be helped. Kirk moved down the right-hand tunnel, slowly and tensely.

The tunnel turned, and Kirk found himself in a small chamber, streaked with bright strata quite unlike the rest of the rock around him. Imbedded in there were dozens of round objects like the one Vanderberg had on his desk, or the one which had so fascinated Spock. He lifted his communicator again. "Mr. Spock."

"Yes, Captain."

"I've found a whole layer of those silicon nodules of yours."

"Indeed, Captain. Most illuminating. Captain—be absolutely certain you do not damage any of them."

"Explain."

"It is only a theory, Captain, but . . ."

His voice was drowned out by the roar of hundreds of tons of collapsing rock and debris. Kirk threw himself against the wall, choking clouds of dust rising around him. When he could see again, it was evident that the roof of the tunnel had fallen across the way he had just come.

"Captain! Are you all right? Captain!"

"Yes, Mr. Spock. Quite all right. But we seem to have had a cave-in."

"I can phaser you out," Spock's voice said.

"No, any disturbance would bring the rest of the wall down. Anyway, it isn't necessary. The chart said our tunnels meet further on. I can just walk out."

"Very well. But I find it disquieting that your roof chose to collapse at that moment. Please proceed with extreme caution. I shall double my pace."

"Very well, Mr. Spock. I'll meet you at the end of the tunnel. Kirk out."

As he tucked the communicator away, there came from behind him a sound as of pebbles being shaken in a can.

He spun instantly, but it was too late. The way was blocked.

It was his first clear sight of the creature, which was reared in the center of the tunnel. It was huge, shaggy, multicolored, and knobby with objects which might have been heads, sense organs, hands—Kirk could not tell. It was quivering gently, still making that strange noise.

Kirk whipped up his phaser. At once the creature shuffled backward. Was it now afraid of just one gun? He raised the weapon again, but this time the creature retreated no further. Neither did it advance.

Phaser at the ready, Kirk moved toward the animal, trying to get around it. At once, it moved to block him—not threateningly, as far as Kirk could tell, but just getting in his way.

Spock chose this moment to call him again. "Captain, a new reading shows the creature . . ."

"I know exactly where the creature is," Kirk said, his phaser steadily on it. "Standing about ten feet away from me."

"Kill it, Captain! Quickly!"

"It's—not making any threatening moves, Mr. Spock."

"You don't dare take the chance! Kill it!"

"I thought you were the one who wanted it kept alive," Kirk said, with grim amusement. "Captured, if possible."

"Your life is in danger, Captain. You can't take the risk."

"It seems to be waiting for something. I want to find out what. I'll shoot if I have to."

"Very well, Captain. I will hurry through my tunnel and approach it from the rear. I remind you that it is a proven killer. Spock out."

The creature was silent now. Kirk lowered his phaser a trifle, but there was no reaction.

"All right," Kirk said. "What do we do now? Talk it over?"

He really had not expected an answer, nor did he get one. He took a step forward and to one side. Again the creature moved to block him; and as it did, Kirk saw along one of its flanks a deep, ragged gouge, leaving a

37

glistening, rocklike surface exposed. It was obviously a wound.

"Well, you can be hurt, can't you?"

He lifted the phaser again. The creature rattled, and shrank back, but held its ground. Obviously it was afraid of the weapon, but it would not flee.

Kirk lowered the phaser, and the rattling stopped. Then he moved deliberately back against the nearest wall and dropped slowly into a squatting position, the phaser held loosely between his knees.

"All right. Your move. Or do we just sit and wait for something to happen?"

It was not a long wait. Almost at once, Spock burst into the area from the open end of the tunnel. He took in the situation instantly and his own phaser jerked up.

"Don't shoot!" Kirk shouted. Echoes went bounding away through the galleries and tunnels.

Spock looked from one to the other. As he did so, the creature moved slowly to the other side of the tunnel. Kirk guessed that he could get past it now before it could block him again. Instead, he said, "Come on over, Mr. Spock."

With the utmost caution, his highly interested eyes fastened on the creature, Spock moved to Kirk's side. He looked up at the walls in which the silicon nodules were imbedded. "Logical," he said.

"But what do they mean?"

"I'd rather not say just yet. If I could possibly get into Vulcan mind-lock with that creature—it would be easier if I could touch it . . ."

Before Kirk could even decide whether to veto this notion, Spock stepped toward the animal, his hand extended. It lurched back at once, its rattling loud and angry-sounding.

"Too bad," Spock said. "But obviously it will permit no contact. Well, then, I must do it the hard way. If you will be patient, Captain . . ."

Spock's eyes closed as he began to concentrate. The intense mental power he was summoning was almost physically visible. Kirk held his breath. The creature twitched nervously, uneasily.

Suddenly Spock's face contorted in agony, and he

38

screamed. "The pain! The pain!" With a great shudder, his face ashen, he began to fall; Kirk got to him just in time.

"Thank—you, Captain," Spock said, gasping and steadying himself. "I am sorry—but that is all I got. Just waves and waves of searing pain. Oh, and a name. It calls itself a Horta. It is in great agony because of the wound—but not reacting at all like a wounded animal."

Abruptly, the creature slithered forward to a smooth expanse of floor, and clung there for a moment. Then it moved away. Where it had been, etched into the floor in still smoking letters, were the words: NO KILL I. Both men stared at the sentence in astonishment.

" 'No kill I' "? Kirk said. "What's that? It could be a plea to us not to kill it—or a promise that it won't kill us."

"I don't know. It appears it learned more from me during our empathy than I did from it. But observe, Captain, that it thinks in vocables. That means it can hear, too."

"Horta!" Kirk said loudly. The creature rattled at once and then returned to silence.

"Mr. Spock, I hate to do this to you, but—it suddenly occurs to me that the Horta couldn't have destroyed that perfusion pump. It was platinum, and immune to the acid mix. It must have hidden it somewhere—and we have to get it back. You'll have to re-establish communications, no matter how painful it is."

"Certainly, Captain," Spock said promptly. "But it has no reason to give us the device—and apparently every reason to wish us off the planet."

"I'm aware of that. If we can win its confidence . . ."

Kirk took out his communicator. "Dr. McCoy. This is the Captain."

"Yes, Captain," McCoy's voice answered.

"Get your medical kit and get down here on the double. We've got a patient for you."

"Somebody injured? How?"

"I can't specify, it's beyond my competence. Just come. Twenty-third level; find us by tricorder. And hurry. Kirk out."

"I remind you, Captain," Spock said. "This is a silicon-based form of life. Dr. McCoy's medical knowledge may be totally useless."

"He's a healer. Let him heal. All right, go ahead, Mr. Spock. Try to contact it again. And try to find out why it suddenly took to murder."

The creature moved nervously as Spock approached it, but did not shy off; it merely quivered, and made its warning pebble-sound. Spock's eyes closed, and the rattling slowly died back.

Kirk's communicator beeped again. "Kirk here."

"Giotto, Captain. Are you all right?"

"Perfectly all right. Where are you?"

"We're at the end of the tunnel. Mr. Vanderberg and his men are here. They're pretty ugly. I thought I'd check with you first . . ."

"Hold them there, Commander. Under no circumstances allow them in here yet. The minute Dr. McCoy gets there, send him through."

"Aye aye, sir. Giotto out."

Spock was now deep in trance. He began to murmur.

"Pain . . . pain . . . Murder . . . the thousands . . . devils . . . Eternity ends . . . horrible . . . horrible . . . in the Chamber of the Ages . . . the Altar of Tomorrow . . . horrible . . . Murderers . . . Murderers . . ."

"Mr. Spock! The pump . . ."

"Stop them . . . kill . . . strike back . . . monsters . . ."

There was the sound of rapidly approaching footsteps and Dr. McCoy, medical bag in hand, broke through into the area. Then he stopped, obviously stunned at what he saw. Kirk silently signaled him to join them, and McCoy, giving the quiescent creature a wide berth, moved to Kirk's side. He said in a low whisper, "What in the name of . . ."

"It's wounded—badly," Kirk whispered back. "You've got to help it."

"Help—*this?*"

"Take a look at it."

McCoy cautiously approached the creature, which was now as immobile as a statue; nor did Spock take any notice.

"The end of life . . . the murderers . . . killing . . . the dead children . . ."

McCoy stared at the gaping wound, and then touched it tentatively here and there. Producing his tricorder, he took a reading, at which he stared in disbelief. Then he came back to Kirk, his face indignant.

"You can't be serious. That thing is virtually made out of stone on the outside, and its guts are plastics."

"Help it. Treat it."

"I'm a doctor, not a bricklayer!"

"You're a healer," Kirk said. "That's your patient. That's an order, Doctor."

McCoy shook his head in wonder, but moved back toward the animal. Spock's eyes were still closed, his face sweating with effort. Kirk went to him.

"Spock. Tell it we're trying to help. A doctor."

"Understood. Understood. It is the end of Life. Eternity stops. Go out. Into the tunnel. To the Passage of Immortality. To the Chamber of the Ages. Cry for the children. Walk carefully in the Vault of Tomorrow. Sorrow for the murdered children. Weep for the crushed ones. Tears for the stolen ones. The thing you search for is there. Go. Go. Sadness for the end of things."

Kirk could not tell whether he was being given directions, or only eavesdropping upon a meditation. He looked hesitantly toward the tunnel entrance.

"Go!" Spock said. "Into the tunnel. There is a small passage. Quickly. Quickly. Sorrow . . . such sorrow. Sadness. Pain." There were tears running down his cheeks now. "Sorrow . . . the dead . . . the children . . ."

Kirk felt a thrill of sympathy. He did not in the least understand this litany, but no one could hear so many emotionally loaded words chanted in circumstances of such tension without reacting.

But the directions turned out to be clear enough. Within a minute he was able to return, the pump in one hand, a silicon nodule in the other.

McCoy was kneeling by the flank of the animal, and speaking into his communicator. "That's right, Lieutenant. Beam it down to me immediately. Never mind what I want it for, I just want it. Move!"

41

"The ages die," Spock said. "It is time to sleep. It is over. Failure. The murderers have won. Death is welcome. Let it end here, with the murdered children . . ."

"Mr. Spock!" Kirk called. "Come back! Spock!"

Spock shuddered with the effort to disengage himself. Kirk carefully put the pump on the floor of the tunnel, then waited until Spock's eyes were no longer glazed.

"I found the unit," Kirk said. "It's in good shape. I also found about a thousand of these silicon balls. They're —eggs, aren't they, Mr. Spock?"

"Yes, Captain. Eggs. And about to hatch."

"The miners must have broken into the hatchery. Their operations destroyed hundreds of them. No wonder . . ."

There was a roar of sound, and Vanderberg, Appel and what seemed to be an army of armed civilians were trying to jam themselves into the tunnel. They shouted in alarm as they saw the creature. Phasers were raised. Kirk jumped forward.

"No!" he shouted. "Don't shoot!"

"Kill it, kill it!" Appel yelled.

Kirk raised his own weapon. "The first man who shoots, dies."

"You can't mean it," Vanderberg said, pointing at the Horta with a finger quivering with hatred. "That thing has killed fifty of my men!"

"And you've killed hundreds of her children," Kirk said quietly.

"What?"

"Those 'silicon nodules' you've been collecting and destroying are eggs. Tell them, Mr. Spock."

"There have been many generations of Horta on this planet," Spock said. "Every fifty thousand years the entire race dies—all but one, like this one. But the eggs live. She protects them, cares for them, and when they hatch, she is the mother to them—thousands of them. This creature here is the mother of her race."

"She's intelligent, peaceful and mild," Kirk added. "She had no objection to sharing the planet with you people— until you broke into the nursery and started destroying her eggs. Then she fought back, in the only way she

42

could—as any mother would—when her children were endangered."

"How were we to know?" Vanderberg said, chastened and stunned. "But—you mean if those eggs hatch, there'll be thousands of them crawling around down here? We've got pergium to deliver!"

"And now you've got your reactor pump back," Kirk said. "She gave it back. You've complained that this planet is a minerological treasure house, if only you had the equipment to get at everything. Well, the Horta moves through rock the way we move through air—and leaves a tunnel. The greatest natural miners in the universe.

"I don't see why we can't make an agreement—reach a *modus vivendi*. They tunnel, you collect and process. You get along together. Your processing operation would be a thousand times more profitable than it is now."

"Sounds all right," Vanderberg said, still a little dubiously. "But how do you know the thing will go for it?"

"Why should it not?" Spock said. "It is logical. But there is one problem. It is badly wounded. It may die."

McCoy rose to his feet, a broad smile on his face. "It won't die. By golly, I'm beginning to think I can cure a rainy day."

"You cured it?" Kirk said in amazement. "How?"

"I had the ship beam down ten pounds of thermo-concrete, the kind we build emergency shelters out of. It's mostly silicon. I just troweled it over the wound. It'll act as a 'bandage' until it heals of itself. Take a look. Good as new."

"Bones, my humblest congratulations. Mr. Spock, I'll have to ask you to get in contact with the Horta again. Tell it our proposition. She and her children make all the tunnels they want. Our people will remove the minerals, and each side will leave the other alone. Think she'll go for it?"

"As I said, Captain, it seems logical. The Horta has a very logical mind." He paused a moment. "And after years of close association with humans, I find it curiously refreshing."

# JOURNEY TO BABEL

## (D. C. Fontana)

The honor guard of eight security men was lined up before the airlock, four men to a side, with Kirk, Spock and McCoy, all three in formal dress blue uniforms, at the end of this human tube. McCoy tugged at his collar, which he had previously described as "like having my neck in a sling." He asked Spock, "How does that Vulcan salute go?"

Spock demonstrated. The gesture was complex and McCoy's attempt to copy it was not very convincing.

The surgeon shook his head. "That hurts worse than the uniform."

The uniforms were the least of their discomforts, Kirk thought a little grimly. They'd soon be out of those, after the formal reception tonight, and the Vulcans were the last group of delegates the *Enterprise* had to pick up. Then would come the trip to the neutral planetoid codenamed "Babel"—a two-week journey with a hundred and fourteen Federation delegates aboard, thirty-two of them ambassadors, half of them mad at the other half, and the whole lot touchier than a raw anti-matter pile over the Coridian question. Now *that* was going to be uncomfortable.

The airlock opened, and the Vulcan Ambassador, Sarek, stepped through. Because of Vulcan longevity, it would have been impossible to guess his age—he looked to be no more than in his late forties—but Kirk knew it to be in fact a hundred and two, which was middle age by Vulcan standards. He was followed, several paces behind, by a woman wearing a traveling outfit with a colorful hooded cloak; she in turn was followed by two Vulcan aides.

Kirk, Spock and McCoy stood at attention as the party walked past the honor guard to the Captain. Spock stepped formally in front of Sarek and gave the complex salute.

"Vulcan honors us with your presence," he said. "We come to serve."

Sarek pointedly ignored him and saluted Kirk instead. When he spoke, his voice was almost without inflection.

"Captain, your service honors us."

"Thank you, Ambassador," Kirk said with a slight bow. "Captain James Kirk. My First Officer, Commander Spock. Dr. McCoy, Chief Medical Officer."

Sarek nodded briefly in turn and indicated the rest of his party. "My aides." He held up his hand, first and second fingers extended. The woman stepped forward and touched her first and second fingers to his. "And Amanda, she who is my wife."

"Captain Kirk," the woman said.

"My pleasure, madam. Ambassador, as soon as you're settled, I'll arrange a tour of the ship. My First Officer will conduct you."

I prefer another guide, Captain," Sarek said.

He was absolutely expressionless, and so was Spock. This snub was just as baffling and even more pointed than before, but it would not be a good idea to offend a ranking ambassador.

"Of course—if you wish. Mr. Spock, we have two hours until we leave orbit. Would you like to beam down and visit your parents?"

There was a slight but noticeable silence. Then Spock said, "Captain—Ambassador Sarek and his wife *are* my parents."

Was I just telling myself, Kirk thought glumly after the first shock, that this trip was going to be just "uncomfortable"?

Upon reflection, Kirk gave himself the job of guiding the tour. He found Spock's mother especially interesting—remarkable, even—though she was hard to study because she habitually walked behind and to the side of any man,

46

her husband most notably. This was a Vulcan ritual to which she had adapted, for Amanda was an Earthwoman; almost everyone in the crew knew that much about Spock.

Though in her late fifties, she was still straight, slim and resilient. She had married a Vulcan and come to live on his world where her human-woman emotions had no place. Kirk strongly suspected that she had not lost any of her human humor and warmth, but that it was buried inside, in deference to her husband's customs and society.

He led them into the Engineering Room. Spock, by now in regular uniform, was working at the computer banks behind the grilled partition.

"This is the engineering section," Kirk told his guests. "There are emergency backup systems for the main controls. We also have a number of control computers here."

Amanda was still behind them and, without Sarek appearing to notice, she moved over to Spock. Out of the corner of his eye, Kirk saw each of them cross hands and touch them, palms out, in a ritual embrace. Then they began to murmur. Spock's face was expressionless, as usual. Once, Amanda shook her head ruefully.

Kirk continued his lecture, hoping to avoid trouble, but Sarek's eyes were as alert as his own. "My wife, attend," the Ambassador said. He held up his first and second fingers. Without a word, Amanda nodded to Spock to excuse herself and obediently moved to Sarek, joining her fingers with his, though Kirk guessed that she was really not much interested in the console and its instruments.

Spock, gathering up a handful of tapes, rose and headed for the door. Kirk had a sudden idea.

"Mr. Spock—a moment, please."

The First Officer turned reluctantly. "Yes, Captain?"

"Ambassador, I'm not competent to explain our computer setup. Mr. Spock, will you do so, please?"

"I gave Spock his first instruction in computers," Sarek said woodenly. "He chose to devote his knowledge to Starfleet rather than the Vulcan Science Academy."

That tore it. In trying to be helpful, Kirk had unwittingly put his foot right into the heart of the family quarrel. Apologetically, he nodded dismissal to Spock, and turned to Sarek.

"I'm sorry, Ambassador. I didn't mean to offend you in . . ."

"Offense is a human emotion, Captain. For other reasons, I am returning to my quarters. Continue, my wife."

Amanda bowed her head in characteristic acceptance, and Sarek left. Kirk, puzzled and confused as never before by his First Officer and his relatives, turned to her, shaking his head.

"I'm afraid I don't understand, Mrs. Sarek."

"Amanda," she said quickly. "I'm afraid you couldn't pronounce the Vulcan family name."

"Can you?"

A smile fluttered on her lips, then vanished as habit overtook her. "After a fashion, and after many years of practice . . . Shall we continue the tour? My husband did request it."

"It sounded more like a command."

"Of course. He's a Vulcan. I'm his wife."

"Spock is his son."

Amanda glanced at him sharply, as though surprised, but recovered quickly. "You don't understand the Vulcan way, Captain. It's logical. It's a better way than ours—but its not easy; It has kept Spock and Sarek from speaking as father and son for eighteen years."

"Spock is my best officer," Kirk said. "And my best friend."

"I'm glad he has such a friend. It hasn't been easy for Spock—neither Vulcan nor human; at home nowhere, except Starfleet."

"I gather Spock disagreed with his father over his choice of a career."

"My husband has nothing against Starfleet. But Vulcans believe peace should not depend on force. Sarek wanted Spock to follow his teaching as Sarek followed the teaching of *his* father."

"And they're both stubborn."

Amanda smiled. "Also a human trait, Captain."

Abruptly, Uhura's voice interrupted from a console speaker. "Bridge to Captain Kirk."

Kirk snapped a toggle. "Kirk here."

"Captain, I've picked up some sort of signal; just a few symbols, nothing intelligible."

"Source?"

"That's what bothers me, sir. Impossible to locate. There wasn't enough of it. Sensors show nothing in the area. But it was a strong signal, as though it was very close."

"Go to alert status four. Begin long-range scanning. Kirk out." Kirk frowned thoughtfully and flicked off the switch. "Madame—Amanda—I'll have to ask you to excuse me. I shall hope to see you again at the reception this evening."

"Certainly, Captain. Both Vulcans and humans know what duty is."

The reception was already going full blast when Kirk arrived. Amid a murmur of conversation, delegates circulated, or sampled the table of exotic drinks, *hors d'oeuvre*. There was a fantastic array of them from many cultures.

Over it all was a faint aura of edgy politeness verging on hostility. The Interplanetary Conference had been called to consider the petition of the Coridian planets to be admitted to the Federation. The Coridian system had already been claimed by some of the races who now had delegates aboard the *Enterprise,* races who therefore had strong personal reasons for keeping Coridan *out* of the Federation. Keeping open warfare from breaking out among the delegates before the Conference even began was going to be a tough problem; many of them were not even trained diplomats, but minor officials who had been handed a hot potato by bosses who did not want to be saddled with the responsibility for whatever happened on Babel.

Kirk spotted Spock and McCoy in a group which included a Tellarite named Gav, two Andorians called Shras and Thelev, and Sarek and Amanda. Well, at least Spock was—er—associating with his family, however distantly.

As Kirk joined the group, McCoy was saying, "Mr. Ambassador, I understood that you had retired from public service before this conference was called. Forgive my curiosity, but, as a doctor, I'm interested in Vulcan physiology. Isn't it unusual for a Vulcan to retire at your age? You're only a hundred or so."

As was characteristic of Andorians because of their sensitive antennae, Shras was listening with his head down and slightly tilted, while Gav, sipping a snifter of brandy, was staring directly into Sarek's face. For an Earthman unaccustomed to either race, it would have been hard to say which of them, if either, was being rude.

Sarek said, "One hundred and two point four three seven, measured in your years. I had other—concerns."

Gav put his snifter down and leaned still farther forward. When he spoke, his voice was rough, grating and clumsy; English was very difficult for all his people, if he spoke it better than most. "Sarek of Vulcan, do you vote to admit Coridan to the Federation?"

"The vote will not be taken here, Ambassador Gav. My government's instructions will be heard in the Council Chamber on Babel."

"No—*you*. How do *you* vote, Sarek of Vulcan?"

Shras lifted his head. "Why must you know, Tellarite?" His voice was whispery, almost silken.

"In Council, his vote carries others," Gav said, stabbing a finger toward Sarek. "I will know where he stands, and why."

"Tellarites do not argue for reasons," Sarek said. "They simply argue."

"That is a . . ."

"Gentlemen," Kirk interrupted firmly. "As Ambassador Sarek pointed out, this is not the Council Chamber on Babel. I'm aware the admission of Coridan is a highly debatable issue, but you can't solve it here."

For a moment the three Ambassadors stared defensively at each other. Then Sarek nodded to Kirk. "You are correct, Captain. Quite logical."

"Apologies, Captain," Shras whispered.

Gav remained rigid for a moment, then nodded and said in an angry voice, "You will excuse me," and left the group.

"You have met Gav before, Ambassador," Shras said softly to Sarek.

"We debated at my last Council session."

"Ambassador Gav lost," Amanda added with a straight face. If Shras was amused, his face was incapable of showing it. He nodded solemnly and moved off.

"Spock, I've always suspected you were more human," McCoy said, in an obvious attempt to lighten the atmosphere. "Mrs. Sarek, I know about the rigorous training of Vulcan boys, but didn't he ever run and play like human youngsters? Even in secret?"

"Well," said Amanda, "he did have a sehlat he was very fond of."

"Sehlat?"

"It's rather like a fat teddy bear."

McCoy's eyes went wide. "A teddy bear?"

Several other crew personnel had overheard this and there was a general snicker. Quickly, Sarek turned to his wife and took her arm firmly.

"Excuse us, Doctor," he said. "It has been a long day for my wife." He propelled her toward the door amid a barrage of "good nights."

McCoy turned back to Spock, who did not appear the least bit discomforted. "A teddy bear!"

"Not precisely, Doctor," Spock said. "On Vulcan, the 'teddy bears' are alive and have six-inch fangs."

McCoy, no Vulcan, was obviously rocked. He was bailed out by a nearby wall communicator, which said in Chekov's voice, "Bridge to Captain Kirk."

"Kirk here."

"Captain, sensors are registering an unidentified vessel pacing us."

"On my way. Duty personnel on yellow alert. Passengers are not to be alarmed . . . Mr. Spock!"

The intruder turned out to be a small ship, about the size of a scout, of no known configuration, and unauthorized in this quadrant. It had been paralleling the course of the *Enterprise* for five minutes, outside phaser range and indeed at the extreme limit of the starship's sensors, and would not answer hails on any frequency or in any language. An attempt to intercept showed the intruder not only more maneuverable than the *Enterprise,* but faster, by a nearly incredible two warps. Kirk ordered full analysis of all sensor readings made during the brief approach, and went back to the reception, leaving Spock in command.

It seemed to be petering out. Gav was still there, sitting isolated, still working on the brandy. If he was trying to get drunk, he was due for a disappointment, Kirk knew; alcohol had no effect on Tellarites except to shorten their already short tempers. Shras and Thelev were also still present, heads down, plus a few other delegates.

Most interestingly, Sarek had returned, by himself. Now why? Had his intent been only to get Amanda off the scene before she could further embarrass their son? There could be no emotional motive behind such a move. What would the logical one be? That whether Sarek approved of Starfleet or not, Spock was an officer in it, and could not function properly if he did not command respect? It seemed as good a guess as any; but Kirk knew that his understanding of Vulcan psychology was, to say the least, insecure.

While he was ruminating, Sarek had gone to a drink dispenser, with the aid of which he seemed to have downed a pill of some kind, and Gav had risen and come up behind him. Sensing trouble, Kirk moved unobtrusively closer. Sure enough, Gav had brought up the Coridan question again.

Sarek was saying; "You seem unable to wait for the Council meeting, Ambassador. No matter. We favor admission."

"You favor? *Why?*"

"Under Federation law, Coridan can be protected—its wealth administered for the benefit of its people."

"It's well for you," Gav said. "Vulcan has no mining interest."

"The Coridians have a nearly unlimited wealth of dilithium crystals, but are underpopulated and unprotected. This invites illegal mining operations."

"Illegal! You accuse us . . .?"

"Of nothing," Sarek said. "But reports indicate your ships have been carrying Coridian dilithium crystals."

"You call us thieves?" Without an instant's warning, Gav leaped furiously forward, grasping for Sarek's throat.

52

Sarek blocked the Tellarite's hands and effortlessly slammed him away, against a table. As Gav started to lunge at Sarek again, Kirk caught him and forced him back. "Lies!" Gav shouted over his shoulder. "You slander my people!"

*"Gentlemen!"* Kirk said.

Gav stopped struggling and Kirk stepped back, glaring coldly at both Ambassadors. "Whatever arguments you have among yourselves are your business," Kirk said. *"My* business is running this ship—and as long as I command it, *there will be order."*

"Of course, Captain," Sarek said.

"Understood," Gav said sullenly after a moment. "But Sarek, there will be payment for your slander."

"Threats are illogical," Sarek said. "And such 'payment' is usually expensive."

However, the fight seemed to be over—and the reception as well. Kirk went to his quarters, almost too tired to worry. It had been a day full of tensions, not one of which was yet resolved. Most of the ship was on night status now, and it was a weary pleasure to go through the silent, empty corridors.

But it was not over yet. In his quarters, he had just gotten out of the dress uniform with relief when his intercom said: "Security to Captain Kirk."

What now? "Kirk here."

"Lt. Josephs, sir. I'm on Deck 11, Section A-3. I just found one of the Tellarites, murdered and stuffed into the Jefferies tube. I think it's the Ambassador himself, sir."

So a part of his mission—to keep the peace on board —had failed already.

McCoy knelt in the corridor next to the Jefferies tube and probed Gav's body, using no instruments but his surgeon's fingers. Kirk and Spock watched; Lt. Josephs and two security guards waited for orders to remove the body. At last McCoy rose.

"How was he killed?" Kirk asked.

"His neck was broken. By an expert."

Spock glanced sharply at McCoy and then bent to examine the body himself. Kirk said, "Explain."

"From the location and nature of the break, I'd say the killer knew exactly where to apply pressure to snap the spine instantly. Not even a blow was used—no bruise."

"Who aboard would have that knowledge besides yourself?"

"Vulcans," Spock said, straightening again. "On Vulcan, the method is called *tal-shaya*—considered a merciful method of execution in ancient times."

"Mr. Spock," Kirk said, "a short time ago I broke up an argument between your father and Gav."

"Indeed, Captain? Interesting."

"Interesting? Spock, do you realize that makes your father the most likely suspect?"

"Vulcans do not approve of violence."

"Are you saying your father couldn't have done this?"

"No," Spock said. "But it would be illogical to kill without reason."

"But it he had such a reason?"

"If there were a reason," Spock said, "my father is quite capable of killing—logically and efficiently. He has the skill, and is still only in middle age."

Kirk stared at his First Officer for a moment, appalled. Then he said, "Come with me. You too, Bones."

He led the way to Sarek's quarters which, he was surprised to see when they were admitted by a smiling Amanda, had not been made up to suit Vulcan taste. He would have thought that Spock would have seen to that. He said, "I'm sorry to disturb you. But I must speak with your husband."

"He's been gone for some time. It's his habit to meditate in private before retiring. What's wrong? Spock?"

At that moment the door opened again and Sarek entered. "You want something of me, Captain?"

Kirk observed that he looked somewhat tense, not exactly with anxiety, but as though he were fighting something back. "Ambassador, the Tellarite Gav has been found murdered. His neck was broken—in what Spock describes as *tal-shaya*."

Sarek glanced at his son, lifting an eyebrow in the same familiar manner. "Indeed? Interesting."

"Ambassador, where were you in the past hour?"

"This is ridiculous, Captain," Amanda said. "You aren't accusing him . . .?"

Spock said, "If only on circumstantial evidence, he is a logical suspect, Mother."

"I quite agree," Sarek said, but he seemed more tense than before. "I was in private meditation. Spock will tell you that such meditation is a personal experience, not to be discussed. Certainly not with Earthmen."

"That's a convenient excuse, Ambassador, but . . ."

He broke off as Sarek gasped and started to crumple. He went to his knees before Kirk and Spock could catch him, clutching at his rib cage. A moan escaped him; any pain that could force such a sound from a Vulcan must have been agonizing indeed.

McCoy took a quick reading, then took out a pressure hypo, set it, and gave Sarek a quick injection. Then he went back to the instruments, taking more time with them now.

"What's wrong?" Amanda asked him.

"I don't know—I can't be sure with Vulcan physiology. It looks like something to do with his cardiovascular system, but . . ."

"Can you help him, Bones?"

"I don't know *that* yet, either."

Kirk looked at mother and son in turn. Spock was as expressionless as always, but Amanda's eyes were haunted; not even years of adaptation to Vulcan tradition could cover a worry of this kind.

"I must go off duty," he told her apologetically. "Still another problem confronts me in the morning, for which I'll need a fresh mind. Should I be needed here before then, Dr. McCoy will of course call me."

"I quite understand, Captain," she said gently. "Good night, and thank you."

A truly remarkable woman.

Not much progress, it turned out on the next trip, had been made on the problem of the ship shadowing the *Enterprise*. Readings taken during the brief attempt at interception showed only that it either had a high-density hull or was otherwise cloaked against sensor probes. It was definitely manned, but by what? The Romulans had nothing like it, nor did the Federation or neutral planets, and that it was Klingon seemed even more unlikely.

Two fragmentary transmissions had been picked up, in an unknown code—with a reception point somewhere inside the *Enterprise* herself. Kirk ordered the locator field tightened to include only the interior of his own ship; if somebody aboard had a personal receiver—as seemed all too likely now—it might be pinned down, *if* the shadow sent another such message.

There seemed to be nothing further to be done on that for the moment. With Spock, whose only concern over his father's illness seemed to be over its possible adverse effect upon the mission, Kirk paid a visit to Sickbay. Sarek was bedded down there, with McCoy and Nurse Christine Chapel trying to make sense of the strange reports the body function panel was giving them; Amanda hovered in the door, trying to keep out of the way. As for Sarek himself, he looked as though he felt inconvenienced, but no longer in uncontrollable pain.

"How is he, Bones?"

"As far as I can tell, our prime suspect has a malfunction in one of the heart valves. I couldn't make a closer diagnosis on a Vulcan without an exploratory. Mrs. Sarek, has he had any previous attacks of this sort?"

"No," Amanda said.

"Yes," Sarek said almost simultaneously. "There were three others. My physician prescribed benjasidrine for the condition."

"Why didn't you tell me?" Amanda asked.

"There was nothing you could have done. The prognosis was not serious, providing I retired, which, of course, I did."

"When did you have these attacks, Ambassador?" McCoy said.

"Two before my retirement. The third, while I was meditating on the Observation Deck when the Tellarite was murdered. I was quite incapacitated."

"I saw you taking a pill not long before that," Kirk said. "If you'll give one to Dr. McCoy for analysis, it should provide circumstantial evidence in your favor. Were there any witnesses to the Observation Deck attack?"

"None. I do not meditate among witnesses."

"Too bad. Mr. Spock, you're a scientist and you know Vulcan. Is there a standard procedure for this condition?"

"In view of its reactivation by Sarek's undertaking this mission," Spock said, "the logical approach would be a cryogenic open-heart operation."

"Unquestionably," Sarek said.

"For that, the patient will need tremendous amounts of blood," McCoy said. "Christine, check the blood bank and see if we've got enough Vulcan blood and plasma. I strongly suspect that we don't have enough even to begin such an operation."

"There are other Vulcans aboard."

"You will find," Sarek said, "that my blood type is T-negative. It is rare. That my two aides should be lacking this factor is highly unlikely."

"I, of course," Spock said, "also have T-negative blood."

"There are human factors in your blood that would have to be filtered out, Mr. Spock," Christine said. "You just couldn't give enough to compensate for that."

"Not necessarily," Spock said. "There is a drug which speeds up replacement of blood in physiologies like ours . . ."

"I know the one you mean," McCoy said. "But it's still experimental and has worked only on a Rigellian. The two physiologies are similar, but not identical. Even with the Rigellian, it put a tremendous strain on the liver and the spleen, to say nothing of the bone marrow—and I'd have to give it to *both* of you. Plus which, I've never operated on a Vulcan. I've studied Vulcan anatomy, but that's a lot different from having actual surgical experience. If I don't kill Sarek with the operation, the drug probably will; it might kill both of them."

Sarek said, "I consider the safety factor to be low, but acceptable."

"Well, I don't," McCoy said, "and in this Sickbay, what I think is law. I can't sanction it."

"And *I* refuse to permit it," Amanda said. "I won't risk both of you . . ."

"You must understand, Mother," Spock said. "The chances of finding sufficient T-negative blood otherwise are vanishingly small. I would estimate them at . . ."

"Please don't," Amanda said.

"Then you automatically condemn Sarek to death," Spock said evenly. "And Doctor, you have no choice either. You must operate, and you have both the drug and a donor."

"It seems the only answer," Sarek said.

Reluctantly, McCoy nodded. Amanda turned a stricken face to Kirk, but he could offer her no help; he could not even help himself in this dilemma.

"I don't like it either, Amanda, believe me," he said. "But we must save your husband. You know very well, too, how much I value your son; but if we must risk him too, then we must. Doctor McCoy has agreed—and I learned long ago never to overrule him in such matters. In fact, I have made him the only officer on the *Enterprise* who has the power to give *me* orders. Please try to trust him as I do."

"And as I do also," Spock said, to McCoy's obvious startlement.

"I'll—try," Amanda said.

"You can do no more. Should you need me, I'll be at my station."

With a great deal more distress than he hoped he had shown, Kirk bowed formally and left.

And halfway to the bridge, deep in thought, he was jumped from behind.

A heavy blow to the head with some sort of club staggered him, but he nevertheless managed to throw his assailant from him against the wall. He got a quick impression of a figure taller but slighter than his own, and the flash of a bladed weapon. In the melee that followed, the other man proved himself to be an experienced infighter, and Kirk was already dazed by the first blow. He managed at last to drop his opponent, perhaps permanently—but not before getting the knife in his own back.

He barely made it to an intercom before losing consciousness.

He came to semiconsciousness to the sound of McCoy's voice.

"It's a bad wound—punctured the left lung. A centimeter or so lower and it would have gone through the heart. Thank goodness he had sense enough not to try to pull the knife out, if he had time to think of it at all."

"The attacker was Thelev. Unconscious, but not seriously injured; just knocked about quite a lot." That was Spock. "He must have caught the Captain by surprise. I'll be in the brig, questioning him, and Shras as well."

"Doctor." This time it was Christine Chapel's voice. "The K-two factor is dropping."

"Spock," McCoy said, "Your father is much worse. There's no longer a choice. I'll have to operate immediately. We can begin as soon as you're prepared."

"No," Spock said.

"What?"

Then came Amanda's voice. "Spock, the little chance your father has depends entirely on you. You volunteered."

"My immediate responsibility is to the ship," Spock said. "Our passengers' safety is, by Starfleet order, of first importance. We are being followed by an alien, possibly hostile ship. I cannot relinquish command under these circumstances."

"You can turn command over to Scott," McCoy said harshly.

"On what grounds, Doctor? Command requirements do not recognize personal privilege. I will be in the brig interrogating the Andorian."

Then the darkness closed down again. When he awoke once more, he felt much better. Opening his eyes, he saw Sarek in the bed beside him, apparently asleep, with McCoy and Christine bending over him.

Kirk tried to rise. The attempt provoked a wave of dizziness and nausea and he promptly lay down again —even before McCoy, who had turned instantly at the motion, had to order him to.

"Let that be a lesson to you," McCoy said. "Just lie there and be happy you're still alive."

"How's Sarek?"

"Not good. If I could only operate . . ."

"What's stopping you? Oh, I remember now. Well, Spock's right, Bones. I can't damn him for his loyalty, or for doing his duty. But I'm not going to let him commit patricide."

He sat up, swinging his feet off the bed. McCoy caught his shoulders, preventing him from rising. "Jim, you can't even stand up. You could start the internal bleeding again."

"Bones, Sarek will die without that operation." McCoy nodded. "And you can't operate without the transfusions from Spock." Again a nod. "I'll convince Spock I'm all right, and order him to report here. Once he's off the bridge, I'll turn command over to Scotty and go to my quarters. Will that fill your prescription?"

"Well, no—but it sounds like the best compromise. Let me give you a hand up."

"Gladly."

McCoy supported him all the way to the bridge, but released him just before the elevator doors snapped open. Spock turned, looking surprised and pleased, but masking it immediately.

"Captain."

Kirk stepped very carefully down to his command chair. He tried to appear as though he were casually surveying the bridge, though in fact he was keeping precarious hold of his balance as spasms of dizziness swept him. McCoy remained glued to his side, but ostentatiously offered him not so much as a hand.

Spock came down into the well of the bridge as Kirk reached his chair and eased himself into it. Kirk smiled and nodded approval.

"I'll take over, Spock. Report to Sickbay with Dr. McCoy."

Spock was studying him closely. Kirk was fighting off the dizziness, at least enough—he hoped—to keep it from showing, but he knew also that he was very pale, about which he could do nothing.

"Captain, are you quite all right?"

"I've certified him physically fit, Mr. Spock," McCoy said testily. "Now, I have an operation to perform. And since both of us are required . . ."

He gestured toward the elevator. Spock hesitated briefly, still studying Kirk, who said kindly, "Get out of here, Spock."

Spock nodded, and left with McCoy with something very like alacrity.

"Mr. Chekov," Kirk said, "what is the status of the intruder ship?"

"No change, sir. Maintaining its distance."

"Any further transmissions, Lt. Uhura?"

"None, sir."

Kirk nodded, relaxed a little—and found that he had to pull himself together sharply as the dizziness returned. "Call Mr. Scott to the bridge . . ."

"Captain," Chekov interrupted. "The alien vessel is moving closer!"

"Belay that last order, Lt. Uhura. I'm staying here." But the dizziness kept coming back. He raised a hand to wipe his brow and found that it was shaking.

"Captain," Uhura said. "I'm picking up the alien signal again. But it's coming from inside the *Enterprise*— from the brig."

"Call Security and order an immediate search of the prisoner. Tell them this time to look for implants."

Hours of weakness seemed to pass before the command communicator buzzed. Lt. Josephs' voice said, "Security, Captain. I had to stun the prisoner. He has some sort of transceiver imbedded in one of his antennae, sir; it broke off in my hand. I didn't know they were that delicate."

"They aren't. Thanks, Lieutenant. Neutralize it and send it to Mr. Scott for analysis. Kirk out."

"Captain," Chekov said. "The alien ship has changed course and speed. Moving directly toward us at Warp Eight."

"Lt. Uhura, tell Lt. Josephs to bring the prisoner to the bridge. Mr. Chekov, deflectors on. Red alert. Phasers stand by for fire on my signal."

"Aye, sir." The alarm began to sound. "Shields on. Phasers manned and ready."

"Take over Spock's scanners. Ensign, take the helm."

A blip appeared in the viewscreen and flashed by. It loomed large for an instant, but it was only a blur at this speed. Suddenly the bridge was slammed and rocked. The *Enterprise* had been hit.

"Damage, Mr. Chekov!"

"None, sir; deflected. Target moving away. Turning now. He's coming around again."

"Fire phasers as he passes, Ensign. Steady . . . Fire!"

Chekov studied the scanner. "Clean miss, sir."

At the same moment, there was another jolt. "Report on their weaponry!"

"Sensors report standard phasers, sir."

Standard phasers. Good. The enemy had more speed, but they weren't giants.

Another wave of weakness passed through him. The *Enterprise* seemed to be standing up so far, but he was none too sure of himself.

"Captain, the intercom is jammed," Uhura said. "All the Ambassadors are asking what's going on."

"Tell them to—tell them to take a good guess, but *clear that board,* Lieutenant!"

The ship shook furiously again.

"Captain," Uhura said, "I've got an override from Dr. McCoy. He says that another shock like that and he may lose both patients."

"Tell him this is probably only the beginning. Mr. Chekov, lock fire control into the computers. Set photon torpedoes two, four and six for widest possible scatter at the three highest intercept probabilities . . ."

The enemy flashed by. The torpedoes bloomed harmlessly on the viewscreen. Another slam. Kirk's head reeled.

"Number four shield has buckled."

"Auxiliary power."

"Sir, Mr. Scott reports auxiliary power is being called upon by Sickbay."

"Divert."

"Switching over—shields firming up. Number four still weak, sir. If they hit us there again, it'll go altogether."

"Set computer to drop to number three and switch auxiliary back to Sickbay if it goes."

"Aye, sir."

Kirk heard the elevator doors open behind him, and then Lt. Josephs and another security guard were hustling Thelev before him, without ceremony. It took Kirk a moment to remember that he had ordered exactly this interruption. He stared harshly at the prisoner.

"Your friends out there are good," he said. "But they'll have to blast this ship to dust to win."

"That was intended from the beginning, Captain," Thelev said. He was, Kirk noted with a certain satisfaction, still rather lumpy from his attempt at killing, an impression heightened by the missing antenna. The small wound there had healed, but it looked more as though it had been a deep cut than the loss of a major organ.

"You're not an Andorian. What did it take to make you over?"

The *Enterprise* rocked again. Chekov said, "Shield four down."

"Damage control procedures, all decks," Kirk said. Then, to Thelev; "That ship out there carries phasers. It's faster than we are, but weapon for weapon, we have it outgunned."

Thelev only smiled. "Have you hit it yet, Captain?"

Another shock, and a heavier one. Chekov said, "Shield three weakening. Shall I redivert auxiliary power, sir?"

This was getting them nowhere; if it continued sheerly as a battle of attrition, the *Enterprise* would lose. And there was the operation to consider.

"Engineering, this is the Captain. Blank out all power on the port side of the ship except for phaser banks. On my signal, cut starboard power. Kirk out." He turned back to Thelev. "Who are you?"

"Find your own answers, Captain. You haven't long to live."

"You're a spy, surgically altered to pass an an Andorian. You were planted in the Ambassador's party to use terror and murder to disrupt us and prepare for this attack."

"Speculation, Captain."

The ship shook again. Chekov said, "Shield three is gone, sir."

"Engineering, blank out starboard power, all decks. Maintain until further orders."

The lights on the bridge went out, except for gleams from the telltales on the panels, and the glow of stars from the viewscreen. In the dimness, Thelev at last looked slightly alarmed. "What are you doing?" he said.

"*You* speculate."

"We're starting to drift, Captain," Chekov said. "Shall I hold her on course?"

"No. Stand by your phasers, Mr. Chekov."

"Aye, sir. Phasers standing by."

A blip of pulsing light again appeared in the screen, slowed down, held steady. Kirk leaned forward intently.

"He's just hovering out there, sir."

"Looking us over," Kirk said. "We're dead—as far as he knows. No starship commander would deliberately expose his ship like this, especially one stuffed with notables —or that's what I hope he thinks."

"Range decreasing. Sublight speed."

"Hold your fire."

"Still closing—range one hundred thousand kilometers —phasers locked on target . . ."

"Fire."

The blip flared brightly on the screen. A jubilant shout went up from Chekov. "Got him!"

"Lt. Uhura, open a hailing frequency. If they wish to surrender . . ."

He was interrupted by a glaring burst of light from the viewscreen. Everyone instinctively ducked; the light was blinding. When Kirk could see the screen again, there was nothing on it but stars.

"They could not surrender, Captain," Thelev said. "The ship had orders to self-destruct."

"Lt. Uhura, relay to Starfleet Command. Tell them we have a prisoner."

"Only temporarily, Captain," Thelev said. "You see, I

had self-destruct orders, too. Slow poison—quite painless, actually, but there is no known antidote. I anticipate another ten minutes of life."

Kirk turned to the security guards. "Take him to Sickbay," he said harshly.

Josephs and the guard came down to flank Thelev, and began to shepherd him toward the elevator. As they reached the door, the spy crumpled, sagged, fell to his knees. He said tonelessly, "I seem to—have—miscalculated . . ."

He fell face down and was still. Kirk rose wearily.

"So did they," he said. "Put him in cold storage for an autopsy. Secure for General Quarters. Mr. Chekov, take over."

He went down to the operating room. It was empty, the operating table clear, the instruments mutely inactive. After a moment, McCoy came in from the Sickbay area. He looked as drawn and tired as Kirk felt.

"Bones?"

"Are you quite through shaking this ship around?" the surgeon asked.

"Sarek—Spock—how are they?"

"I don't mind telling you, you make things difficult for a surgeon conducting a delicate operation which . . ."

*"Bones."*

The Sickbay doors opened again and Amanda appeared. "Captain, come in," she said. Kirk shoved past McCoy eagerly.

Inside, Sarek and Spock occupied two of the three beds, side by side. Both looked pale and exhausted, but reasonably chipper. Amanda sat down happily beside Sarek.

"That pigheaded Vulcan stamina," McCoy's voice said behind him. "I couldn't have pulled them through without it."

"Some doctors have all the luck."

"Captain," Spock said. "I believe the alien . . ."

"We damaged their ship," Kirk said. "They destroyed it to avoid capture. Bones, Thelev's body is being brought to your lab. I want an autopsy as soon as you feel up to it."

"I believe you'll find he's what's usually called an Orion, Doctor," Spock said. "There are intelligence reports that

Orion smugglers have been raiding the Coridian system."

"But what could they gain by an attack on us?" Kirk asked.

"Mutual suspicion," Sarek suggested, "and perhaps interplanetary war."

Kirk nodded. "With Orion carefully neutral. She'd clean up by supplying dilithium to both sides—and continue to raid Coridan."

"It was the power utilization curve that confused me," Spock said. "I did not realize that until I was just going under the anesthetic. The curve made it appear more powerful than a starship—than anything known to us. That ship was constructed for a suicide mission. Since they never intended to return to base, they could utilize one hundred per cent power in their attacks. I cannot understand why I didn't realize that earlier."

Kirk looked at Sarek. "You might have had a few other things on your mind."

"That does not seem likely."

"No," Kirk said wryly. "But thank you anyway."

"And you, Sarek," Amanda said. "Would you also say thank you to your son?"

"I do not understand."

"For saving your life."

"Spock behaved in the only logical manner open to him," Sarek said. "One does not thank logic, Amanda."

Amanda stiffened and exploded. "Logic! Logic! I am sick to death of logic. Do you want to know how I feel about your logic?"

The two Vulcans studied the angry woman as though she were some sort of exhibit. Spock glanced at his father and said, quite conversationally, "Emotional, isn't she?"

"She has always been that way."

"Indeed? Why did you marry her?"

"At the time," Sarek said solemnly, "it seemed the logical thing to do."

Amanda stared at them, stunned. Kirk could not help grinning, and McCoy was grinning, too. Amanda, turning to them in appeal, was startled; and then, obviously, suddenly realized that her leg was being pulled. A smile broke over her face.

Equally suddenly, the room reeled. Kirk grabbed the edge of the table. Instantly, McCoy was beside him, guiding him toward the third bed.

"Bones—really—I'm all right."

"If you keep arguing with your kindly family doctor, you'll spend the next ten days right here. Cooperate and you'll get out in two."

Kirk subsided, but now Spock was sitting up. "If you don't mind, Doctor, I'll report to my own station now."

McCoy pointed firmly at the bed. "You're at your station, Spock."

The First Officer shrugged and settled back. McCoy surveyed his three restive patients with an implacable expression.

"Bones," Kirk said, "I think you're enjoying this."

"Indeed, Captain," Spock agreed. "I've never seen him look so happy."

"Shut up," McCoy commanded. There was a long silence. McCoy's expression gradually changed to one of incredulity.

"Well, what do you know?" he said to Amanda. "I finally got the last word!"

# THE MENAGERIE*

## (Gene Roddenberry)

When the distress signal from Talos IV came through, via old-fashioned radio, Captain Christopher Pike was of two minds about doing anything about it. The message said it was from survivors of the SS *Columbia,* and a library search by Spock showed that a survey ship of that name had indeed disappeared in that area—eighteen years ago. It had taken all of those years for the message, limited to the speed of light, to reach the *Enterprise,* which passed through its wave-front just slightly eighteen light-years from the Talos system. A long time ago, that had been.

In addition, Pike had his own crew to consider. Though the *Enterprise* had come out of the fighting around Rigel VIII—her maiden battle—unscarred, the ground skirmishing had not been as kind to her personnel. Spock, for example, was limping, though he was trying to minimize it, and Navigator Jose Tyler's left forearm was bandaged

---

*As originally produced, this story ran in two parts. The main story, which takes place so far back in the history of the *Enterprise* that the only familiar face aboard her then was Spock, appeared surrounded by and intercut with an elaborate "framing" story, in which Spock is up for court-martial on charges of mutiny and offers the main story as an explanation of his inarguably mutinous behavior. Dramatically, this was highly effective—indeed, as I've already noted, it won a "Hugo" award in this category for that year—but told as fiction, it involves so many changes of viewpoint, as well as so many switches from present to past, that it becomes impossibly confusing. (I know—I've tried!) Hence the present version adapts only the main story, incidentally restoring to it the ending it had—never shown on television—before the frame was grafted onto it. I think the producers also came to feel that the double-plotted version had been a mistake; at least, "The Menagerie" turned out to be the only two-part episode in the entire history of the series. —J.B.

down to his palm. Pike himself was unhurt, but he felt desperately tired.

Nevertheless, the library also reported Talos IV to be habitable, so survivors from the *Columbia* might still be alive; and since the *Enterprise* would be passing within visual scanning distance anyhow, it wouldn't hurt to take a look. The chances of finding anything at this late date . . .

But almost at once, Tyler picked up reflections from the planet's surface whose polarization and scatter pattern indicated large, rounded chunks of metal, which might easily have been parts of a spaceship's hull. Pike ordered the *Enterprise* into orbit.

"I'll want a landing party of six, counting myself. Mr. Tyler, you'll be second in command, and we'll need Mr. Spock too; both of you, see that there's a fresh dressing on your wounds. Also, Dr. Boyce, Chief Garrison and ship's geologist. Number One, you're in command of the *Enterprise* in our absence. Who seconds you now?"

"Yeoman Colt, sir."

Pike hesitated. That this left the bridge dominated by women didn't bother him; female competence to be in Star Fleet had been tested and proven before he had been born. And Pike had the utmost confidence in Number One, ordinarily the ship's helmsman and, after the Rigel affair, the most experienced surviving officer. Slim and dark in a Nile Valley sort of way, she was one of those women who always look the same between the ages of twenty and fifty, but she had a mind like the proverbial steel trap and Pike had never seen her shaken in any situation. Yeoman Colt, however, was a recent replacement, and an unknown quantity. Well, the assignment was likely to prove a routine one, anyhow.

"Very well. We'll beam down to the spot where Mr. Tyler picked up those reflections."

This proved to be on a rocky plateau, not far from an obvious encampment—a rude collection of huts, constructed out of slabs of rock, debris from a spaceship hull, scraps of canvas and other odds and ends. Several fairly old men

70

were visible, all bearded, all wearing stained and tattered garments. One was carrying water; the others were cultivating a plot of orange vegetation. The ingenuity and resolute will which had enabled them to exist for nearly two decades on this forbidding alien world were everywhere evident.

One of them looked up in the direction of the landing party and froze, clearly unable to believe his eyes. At last he called hoarsely, "Winter! *Look!*"

A second man looked up, and reacted almost as the first had. Then he shouted; "They're men! Human!"

The sound of their voices brought other survivors out of their huts and sheds. The youngest looked to be nearly fifty, but they were tanned, hardened, in extraordinarily good health. The two groups approached each other slowly, solemnly; Pike could almost feel the intensity of emotion. He stepped forward and extended a hand.

"Captain Christopher Pike, United Spaceship *Enterprise.*"

The first survivor to speak mutely accepted Pike's hand, tears on his face. At last he said, with obvious effort, "Dr. Theodore Haskins, American Continent Institute."

"They're *men!* Here to take us back!" the man called Winter said, laughing with sudden relief. "You are, aren't you? Is Earth all right?"

"Same old Earth," Pike said, smiling. "You'll see it before long."

"And you won't believe how fast you can get back," Tyler added. "The time barrier's been broken! Our new ships can . . ."

He broke off, mouth open, staring past Haskins' shoulder. Following the direction of the navigator's gaze, Pike saw standing in a hut doorway a remarkably beautiful young woman. Although her hair was uncombed and awry, her makeshift dress tattered, she looked more like a woodland nymph than the survivor of a harrowing ordeal. Motioning her forward, Haskins said, "This is Vina. Her parents are dead; she was born almost as we crashed."

There were more introductions all around, but Pike found himself almost unable to take his eyes off the girl. Perhaps it was only the contrast she made with the older men, but her young, animal grace was striking. No wonder Tyler had stared.

"No need to prolong this," Pike said. "Collect what personal effects you want to keep and we'll be off. I suggest you concentrate on whatever records you have; the *Enterprise* is amply stocked with necessities, and even some luxuries."

"Extraordinary," Haskins said. "She must be a very big vessel."

"Our largest and most modern type; the crew numbers four hundred and thirty."

Haskins shook his head in amazement and bustled off. Amidst all the activity, Vina approached Pike and drew him a little to one side.

"Captain, may I have a word?"

"Of course, Vina."

"Before we go, there is something you should see. Something of importance."

"Very well. What is it?"

"It's much easier to show than to explain. If you'll come this way . . ."

She led him to a rocky knoll some distance from the encampment, and pointed to the ground at its base. "There it is."

Pike did not know what he had expected—anything from a grave to some sort of alien artifact—but in fact he saw nothing of interest at all, and said so. Vina looked disappointed.

"The angle of the light is probably wrong," she said. "Come around to this side."

They changed places, so that his back was to the knoll, hers to the encampment. As far as Pike could tell, this made no difference.

"I don't understand," he said.

"You will," Vina said, the tone of her voice changing suddenly. "You're a perfect choice."

Pike looked up sharply. As he did so, the girl vanished. It was not the fading dematerialization of the Transporter effect; she simply blinked out as though someone had snapped off a light. With her went all the survivors and their entire encampment, leaving nothing behind but the bare plateau and the stunned men from the *Enterprise*.

There was a hiss behind him and he spun, reaching for his phaser. A cloud of white gas was rolling toward him, through which he could see an oddly shaped portal which, perfectly camouflaged as a part of the rock, had noiselessly opened to reveal the top of a lift shaft. He had an instant's impression of two occupants—small, slim, pale, human-like creatures with large elongated heads, in shimmering metallic robes; one of them was holding a small cylinder which was still spitting the white spray.

In the same instant, the gas hit him and he was para-lyzed, still conscious but unable to move anything but his eyes. The two creatures stepped forward and dragged him into the opening.

*"Captain!"* Spock's voice shouted in the distance. Then there was the sound of running, suddenly muffled as though the doors had closed again, and then the lift dropped with a hissing *whoosh* like that of a high-speed pneumatic tube. Above, and still more distantly, came the sound of a rock explosion as someone fired a phaser at full power, but the lift simply fell faster.

With it, Pike fell into unconsciousness.

He awoke clawing for his own phaser, a spongelike sur-face impeding his movements. The gun was gone. Rolling to his feet, he looked around, at the same time reaching next for his communicator. That was gone too; so was his jacket.

He was in a spotless utilitarian enclosure. The spongy surface turned out to belong to a plastic shape, apparently a sort of bed, with a filmy metallic-cloth blanket folded on it. There was also a free-form pool of surging water, with a small drinking container sitting on the floor next to it. A prison cell, clearly; the bars . . .

But there were no bars. The fourth wall was made up entirely of a transparent panel. Pike hurried to it and peered through. He found himself looking up and down a long corridor, faced with similar panels; but they were off-set to, rather than facing each other, so that Pike could see into only small angled portions of the two nearest him on the other side.

Some sound he had made must have penetrated into the corridor, for suddenly there was a wild snarl, and in the cell—cage?—to his left, a flat creature, half anthropoid, half spider, rushed hungrily at him, only to be thrown back, its ugly fangs clattering against the transparency. Startled, Pike looked to the right; in this enclosure he could see a portion of some kind of tree. Then there was a leathery flapping, and an incredibly thin humanoid/bird creature came into view, peering curiously but shyly toward Pike's cage. The instant it saw Pike watching, it whirled and vanished.

As it did, a group of the pale, large-headed men like those who had kidnapped him came into view, coming toward him. They were lead by one who wore an authoritative-looking jeweled pendant on a short chain around his neck. They all came to a halt in front of Pike's cage, silently watching him. He studied them in turn. They were quite bald, all of them, and each had a prominent vein across his forehead.

Finally, Pike said, "Can you hear me? My name is Christopher Pike, commander of the vessel *Enterprise* of the United Federation of Planets. Our intentions are peaceful. Can you understand me?"

The large forehead vein of one of the Talosians pulsed strongly and, although Pike could see no lip movement, a voice sounded in his head, a voice that sounded as though it were reciting something.

"It appears, Magistrate, that the intelligence of the specimen is shockingly limited."

Now the forehead of the creature with the pendant pulsed. "This is no surprise, since his vessel was lured here so easily with a simulated message. As you can read in its thoughts, it is only now beginning to suspect that the survivors and the encampment were a simple illusion we placed in their minds. And you will note the confusion as it reads our thought transmissions . . ."

"All right, telepathy," Pike broke in. "You can read my mind, I can read yours. Now, unless you want my ship to consider capturing me an unfriendly act . . ."

74

"You now see the primitive fear-threat reaction. The specimen is about to boast of his strength, the weaponry of his vessel, and so on." As Pike stepped back a pace and tensed himself, the Magistrate added, "Next, frustrated into a need to display physical prowess, the creature will throw himself against the transparency."

Pike, his act predicted in mid-move, felt so foolish that he canceled it, which made him angrier than ever. He snarled, "There's a way out of every cage, and I'll find it."

"Despite its frustration, the creature appears more adaptable than our specimens from other planets," the Magistrate continued. "We can soon begin the experiment."

Pike wondered what they meant by *that,* but it was already obvious that they were not going to pay any attention to anything he said. He began to pace. The telepathic "voices" continued behind him.

"Thousands of us are now probing the creature's thoughts, Magistrate. We find excellent memory capacity."

"I read most strongly a recent struggle in which it fought to protect its tribal system. We will begin with this, giving the specimen something more interesting to protect."

The cage vanished.

He was standing alone among rocks and strange vegetation which, on second look, proved to be vaguely familiar. Then an unmistakably familiar voice sounded behind him.

"Come. Hurry!"

He turned to see Vina, her hair long and in braids, dressed like a peasant girl of the terrestrial Middle Ages. Behind her towered a fortress which he might have taken as belonging to the same period had he not recognized it instantly. The girl pointed to it and said, "It is deserted. There will be weapons, perhaps food."

"This is Rigel VIII," Pike said slowly. "I fought in that fortress just two weeks ago. But where do you fit in?"

There was a distant bellowing sound. Vina started,

then began walking rapidly toward the fortress. Pike remained where he was.

*I was in a cell, a cage in some kind of zoo. I'm still there. I just think I see this. They must have reached into my mind, taken the memory of somewhere I've been, something that's happened to me—except that she wasn't in it then.*

The bellowing sounded again, nearer. Pike hurried after the girl, catching up with her just inside the gateway to the fortress' courtyard. The place was a scatter of battered shields, lance staves, nicked and snapped swords; there was even a broken catapult—the debris that had been left behind after Pike's own force had breached and reduced the fortress. Breaking the Kalars' hold over their serfs had been a bloody business, and made more so by the hesitancy of Starfleet Command over whether the whole operation was not in violation of General Order Number One. Luckily, the Kalars themselves had solved that by swarming in from Rigel X in support of their degenerate colony . . .

And that animal roar of rage behind them could only be a stray Kalar colonist, seeking revenge for the fall of his fortress and his feudalism upon anything in his path. Vina was looking desperately for a weapon amid the debris, but there was nothing here she could even lift.

Then the bellow sounded at the gateway. Vina shrank into the nearest shadow, pulling Pike with her. He was in no mood to hang back; memory was too strong. The figure at the courtyard entry was a local Kalar warrior, huge, hairy, Neanderthal, clad in cuirass and helmet and carrying a mace. It looked about, shoulders hunched.

"What nonsense," Pike said under his breath. "It was all over weeks ago . . ."

*"Hush,"* Vina whispered, terrified. "You've been here —you know what he'll do to us."

"It's nothing but a damn silly illusion."

The warrior roared again, challengingly, raising tremendous echoes. Apparently he hadn't seen them yet.

"It doesn't matter *what* you call this," Vina whispered again. "You'll feel it, that's what matters. You'll feel every moment of whatever happens. I'll feel it happening too."

The warrior moved tentatively toward them. Either in genuine panic or to force Pike's hand, Vina whirled and raced for a parapet stairway behind them which lead toward the battlement above. The Kalar spotted her at once; Pike had no choice but to follow.

At the top was another litter of weapons; Vina had already picked up a spear with a head like an assegai. Pike found himself a shield and an unbroken sword. As he straightened, the girl pushed him aside. A huge round rock smashed into the rampart wall inches away from him, the force of the fragments knocking him down.

The pain was real, all right. He raised a hand to his forehead to find it bleeding. Below, the warrior was picking up another rock from a depleted pile on the other side of the catapult.

While Pike scrambled back, Vina threw her spear, but she did it inexpertly, and in any event her strength proved insufficient for the range. Changing his mind at once, the Kalar dropped the stone and came charging up the stairs.

Pike's shield was almost torn from his arm at the first blow of the mace. His own sword clanged harmlessly against the Kalar's armor, and he was driven back by a flurry of blows.

Then there was a twanging sound. The warrior bellowed in pain and swung around, revealing an arrow driven deep into his back. Vina had found a crossbow, cocked and armed, and at that range she couldn't miss.

But the wound wasn't immediately mortal and she obviously did not know how to cock the weapon again. The Kalar, staggering, moved in upon her.

From that close, a crossbow bolt would go through almost any armor, but Pike's sword certainly wouldn't. Dropping it, he sprang forward, raised his shield high, and brought it down with all his strength on the back of the warrior's neck. The creature spun off the rampart edge and plummeted to the floor of the compound below. It struck supine and lay still.

Vina, sobbing with relief, threw herself into Pike's arms . . .

. . . and they were back in the menagerie cage.

She was now wearing her own, shorter hair, and a

simple garment of the metallic Talosian material. His own bruises and exhaustion had vanished completely, along with the shield. It took him a startled moment to realize what had happened.

Vina smiled. "It's over."

"Why are you here?" he demanded.

She hesitated slightly, then smiled again. "To please you."

"Are you real?"

"As real as you wish."

"That's no answer," he said.

"Perhaps they've made me up out of dreams you've forgotten."

He pointed to her garment. "And I dreamed of you in the same metal fabric they wear?"

"I must wear something." She came closer. "or must I? I can wear anything you wish, be anything you wish . . ."

"To make this 'specimen' perform for them? To watch how I react? Is that it?"

"Don't you have a dream, something you've wanted very badly . . ."

"Do they do more than just watch me?" he asked. "Do they *feel* with me too?"

"You can have any dream you wish. I can become anything. Any woman you ever imagined." She tried to nestle closer. "You can go anyplace, do anything—have any experience from the whole universe. Let me please you."

Pike eyed her speculatively. "You can," he said abruptly. "Tell me about them. Is there some way I can keep them from using my own thoughts against me? Ah, you're frightened. Does that mean there *is* a way?"

"You're being a fool."

He nodded. "You're right. Since you insist you're an illusion, there's not much point in this conversation."

He went over to the bed and lay down, ignoring her. It was not hard to sense her anxiety, however. Whatever her task was, she did not want to fail it.

After a while she said, "Perhaps—if you asked me something I could answer . . ."

He sat up. "How far can they control my mind?"

"That's not a—that is—" she paused. "If I tell you—will you pick some dream you've had, let me live it with you?"

Pike considered this. The information seemed worth the risk. He nodded.

"They—they can't actually make you do anything you don't want to."

"They have to try to trick me with their illusions?"

"Yes. And they can punish when you're not cooperative. You'll find out about that."

"They must have lived on the planet's surface once . . ."

"Please," she interrupted. "If I say too much . . ."

"Why did they move underground?" he pressed insistently.

"War, thousands of centuries ago," she said hurriedly. "The ones left on the surface destroyed themselves and almost their whole world too. It's taken that long for the planet to heal itself."

"And I suppose the ones who came underground found life too limited—so they concentrated on developing their mental power."

She nodded. "But they've found it's a trap. Like a narcotic. When dreams become more important than reality, you give up travel, building, creating, you even forget how to repair the machines left behind by your ancestors. You just sit living and reliving other lives in the thought records. Or probe the minds of zoo specimens, descendants of life they brought back long ago from all over this part of the galaxy."

Pike suddenly understood. "Which means they had to have more than one of each animal."

"Yes," Vina said, clearly frightened now. "Please, you said if I answered your questions . . ."

"But that was a bargain with something that didn't exist. You said you were an illusion, remember."

*"I'm a woman,"* she said, angry now. "As real and human as you are. We're—like Adam and Eve. If they can . . ."

She broke off with a scream and dropped to the floor, writhing.

79

"Please!" she wailed. "Don't punish me—I'm trying my best with him—no, *please* . . ."

In the midst of her agony, she vanished. Pike looked up to see the creature called the Magistrate watching through the panel. Furiously, he turned his back—and noticed for the first time an almost invisible circular seam, about man-high, in the wall beside his bed. Was there a hidden panel there?

A small clink of sound behind him made him turn again. A vial of blue liquid was sitting on the floor, just inside the transparency. The Magistrate continued to watch; his mental speech said, "The vial contains a nourishing protein complex."

"Is the keeper actually communicating with one of his animals?"

"If the form and color are not appealing, it can appear as any food you wish to visualize."

"And if I prefer—" Pike began.

"To starve? You overlook the unpleasant alternative of punishment."

With the usual suddenness, Pike found himself writhing in bubbling, sulphurous brimstone in a dark place obscured by smoke. Flame licked at him from all sides. The instant agony was as real as the surprise, and a scream was wrenched from him.

It lasted only a few seconds and then he was back in the cage, staggering.

"From a fable you once heard in childhood," the Magistrate said. "You will now consume the nourishment."

"Why not just put irresistable—hunger in my mind?" Pike said, still gasping with remembered pain. "You can't —do that. You do have limitations, don't you?"

"If you continue to disobey, deeper in your mind there are things even more unpleasant."

Shakily, Pike picked up the vial and swallowed its contents. Almost simultaneously he tossed the vial aside and threw himself at the transparency. It bounced him back, of course—but the Magistrate had also stepped back a pace.·

"That's very interesting," Pike said. "You were startled. Weren't you reading my mind then?"

"Now, to the female. As you have conjectured, an Earth vessel did actually crash on our planet. But with only a single survivor."

"Let's stay on the first subject. All I wanted for that moment was to get my hands around your neck. Do primitive emotions put up a block you can't read through?"

"We repaired the survivor's injuries and found the species interesting. So it became necessary to attract a mate."

"All right, we'll talk about the girl. You seem to be going out of your way to make her seem attractive, to make me feel protective."

"This is necessary in order to perpetuate the species."

"That could be done medically, artificially," Pike said. "No, it seems more important to you now that I accept her, begin to like her . . ."

"We wish our specimens to be happy in their new life."

"Assuming that's another lie, why would you want me attracted to her? So I'll feel love, a husband-wife relationship? That would be necessary only if you needed to build a family group, or even a whole human . . ."

"With the female now properly conditioned, we will continue with . . ."

"You mean properly punished!" Pike shouted. "I'm the one who's not cooperating. Why don't you punish me?"

"First an emotion of protectiveness, now one of sympathy. Excellent." The Magistrate turned and walked away down the corridor. Frustrated again, Pike turned to study the mysterious seam.

He found himself studying a tree instead. Around him, in full day, was richly planted park and forest land, with a city on the horizon. He recognized the place instantly.

Immediately to his right was tethered a pair of handsome saddle horses. To the left, Vina, in casual Earth garb, was laying out a picnic lunch on the grass.

Looking up at him, smiling, she said, "I left the thermos hooked to my saddle."

Pike went to the horses and patted them. "Tango! You

81

old quarter-gaited devil, you! Hello, Mary Lou! No, sorry, no sugar this time . . ."

But patting his pockets automatically, he was astonished to find the usual two sugar cubes there. He fed them to the horses. The Talosians seemed to think of everything.

He unhooked the thermos, carried it to the picnic and sat down, eyeing Vina curiously. She seemed nervous.

"Is it good to be home?" she asked him.

"I've been aching to be back here. They read our minds very well."

"*Please!*" It was a cry of fear. Her face pleaded with him to keep silent.

"Home, everything else I want," he said. "*If* I cooperate. Is that it?"

"Have you forgotten my—headaches, darling? The doctor said when you talk strangely like this . . ."

Her voice trailed off, shaken. Pike was beginning to feel trapped again.

"Look, I'm sorry they punish you," he said. "But I can't let them hold that over our heads. They'll *own* us then."

She continued to lay out the lunch, trying to ignore him. "My, it turned out to be a beautiful day, didn't it?"

"Funny," he mused. "About twenty-four hours ago I was telling the ship's doctor how much I wanted—something not so far from what's being offered here. No responsibility, no frustrations or bruises . . . And now that I have it, I understand the doctor's answer. You either *live* life, bruises and all, or you turn your back on it and start dying. The Talosians went the second way."

"I hope you're hungry," Vina said, with false brightness. "The white sandwiches are your mother's chicken-tuna recipe."

He tried one. She was right. "Doc would be happy about part of this, at least. Said I needed a rest."

"This is a lovely place to rest."

"I spent my boyhood here. Doesn't compare with the gardens around the big cities, but I liked it better." He nodded toward the distant skyline. "That's Mojave. I was born there."

Vina laughed. "Is that supposed to be news to your

wife? See—you're home! You can even stay if you want. Wouldn't it be nice showing your children where you once played?"

"These—'headaches,'" Pike said. "They'll be hereditary. Would you wish them on a child—or a whole group of children?"

"That's foolish."

"Is it? Look, first I'm made to protect you, then to feel sympathy for you—and now familiar surroundings, comfortable husband and wife feelings. They don't need all this just for passion. They're after respect, affection, mutual dependence—and something else . . ."

"They say, in the old days all this was a desert. Blowing sand, cactus . . ."

"I can't help either of us if you won't give me a chance!" Pike said sharply. "You told me once that illusions have become like a narcotic to them. They've even forgotten how to repair the machines left by their ancestors. Is that why we're so important? To build a colony of slaves who can . . ."

"Stop it, stop it! Don't you care what they do to me?"

"There's no such thing as a perfect prison," Pike said. "There's always some way out. Back in my cage, it seemed for a couple of minutes our keeper couldn't read my thoughts. Do emotions like anger block off our thought from them?"

"Don't you think," Vina said angrily, "that I've already tried things like that?"

"There's *some* way to beat them. Answer me!"

Her anger turned to tears. "Yes, they can't read—through primitive emotions. But you can't keep it up long enough. I've tried!" She began to sob. "They—keep at you and—at you, year after year—probing, looking for a weakness, and tricking—and punishing and—they've won. They own me. I know you hate me for it."

Her fear, desperation, loneliness, everything that she had undergone were welling up in misery, deep and genuine. He put an arm around her. "I don't hate you. I can guess what it was like."

"It's not enough! They want you to have feelings that would build a family, protect it, work for it. Don't you

83

understand? They read my thoughts, my desires, my dreams of what would be a perfect man. That's why they picked you. *I can't help but love you.* And they expect you to feel the same way."

Pike was shaken despite himself. The story was all too horribly likely. "If they can read my mind, they know I'm attracted to you. From the first day in the survivor's encampment. You were like a wild little animal."

"Was that the reason? Because I was like a barbarian?"

"Perhaps," Pike said, amused.

"I'm beginning to see why none of this has really worked on you," Vina said, straightening. "You've *been* home. And fighting, like on Rigel, that's not new to you either. A person's strongest dreams are about things he *can't* do."

"Maybe so. I'm no psychologist."

"Yes," she said, smiling, almost to herself. "A ship's captain, always having to be so formal, so decent and honest and proper—he must wonder what it would be like to forget all that."

The scene changed, with a burst of music and wild merriment. The transition caught him still seated. He was now on a pillowed floor at a low round table bearing a large bowl of fruit and goblets of wine. He seemed to be clad now in rich silk robes, almost like that of an Oriental potentate; near him sat a man whom he vaguely remembered as an Earth trader, similarly but less luxuriantly garbed, while on the other side was an officer in Starfleet uniform whom he did not recognize at all. All of them were being served by women whose garb and manner strongly suggested slavery, and whose skins were the same color as Spock's. The music was coming from a quartet seated near a fountain pool.

Again he recognized the place; it was the courtyard of the Potentate of Orion. The officer leaned forward.

"Say, Pike," he said. "You used to be Captain of the *Enterprise,* didn't you?"

"Matter of fact, he was," said the trader.

"Thought so. You stopped here now and then—to check things out, so to speak."

"And then," the trader added, "sent Earth a blistering report on 'the Orion traders taking shocking advantage of the natives.' "

Both men laughed. "Funny how they are on this planet," the officer said. "They actually like being taken advantage of."

"And not just in profits, either."

The officer looked around appraisingly. "Nice place you've got here, Mr. Pike."

"It's a start," the trader said. Both laughed again. The officer patted the nearest slave girl on the rump.

"Do any of you have a green one?" he asked. "They're dangerous, I hear. Razor-sharp claws, and they attract a man like a sensation of irresistible hunger."

Up to now, the officer had simply repelled Pike, but that last phrase sounded familiar—and had been delivered with mysterious emphasis. The trader gave Pike a knowing look.

"Now and then," he said, "comes a man who tames one."

There was a change in the music; it became louder, took on a slow, throbbing rhythm. The slave girls turned hurriedly, as if suddenly anxious to excape. Looking toward the musicians, Pike saw another girl, nude, her skin green, and glistening as if it had been oiled, kneeling at the edge of the pool. Her fingertips were long, gleaming, razor-edged scimitars; her hair like the mane of a wild animal. She was staring straight at him.

One of the slaves was slow. The green girl sprang up with a sound like a spitting cat, barring her escape. A man Pike had not seen before leapt forward to intervene, raising a whip.

"Stop!" Pike shouted, breaking his paralysis. The green girl turned and looked at him again, and then he recognized her. It was Vina once more.

She came forward to the center of the rectangle and posed for a moment. Then the music seemed to reach her, the slow surging beat forcing movement out of her as a reed flute takes possession of a cobra. She threw her head back, shrieked startlingly, and began to dance.

"Where'd he find her?" said the officer's voice. Pike was unable to tear his eyes away from her.

"He'd stumbled into a dark corridor," the trader's voice said, "and then he saw flickering light ahead. Almost like secret dreams a bored sea captain might have, wasn't it? There she was, holding a torch, glistening green . . ."

"Strange looks she keeps giving you, Pike."

"Almost as if she knows something about you."

Somewhere in the back of his mind he knew that the Talosians were baiting him through these two men; but he could not stop watching the dance.

"Wouldn't you say that's worth a man's soul?" said the trader.

"It makes you believe she could be anything," said the officer. "Suppose you had all of space to choose from, and this was only one small sample . . ."

That was too much. Pike rose, growling. "Get out of my way, blast you!"

He crossed the courtyard to a curtained doorway which he seemed to recall was an exit. Brushing the curtains aside, he found himself in a corridor. It was certainly dark, and grew darker as he strode angrily along it. In the distance was a flickering light, and then, there indeed was Vina, holding aloft a torch . . .

The scene lightened and the torch vanished. Vina, her skin white, her body covered with the Talosian garment, continued to hold her empty hand aloft for a second. They were back in the cage.

Vina's face contorted in fury. She ran to the transparency and pounded on it, shouting out into the corridor.

"No! Let us finish! I could have . . ."

"What's going on here?" another woman's voice demanded. Both Pike and Vina whirled.

There were two other women in the cage: Number One, and Yeoman Colt. After so many shocks, Pike could summon no further reaction to this one.

"I might well ask you the same thing," he said numbly.

"We tried to Transport down in here," Number One said. "There was a risk we'd materialize in solid rock, but we'd already tried blasting open the top of the lift, with no luck."

"But there were six of us to start with," Yeoman Colt said. "I don't know why the others didn't make it."

"It's not fair!" Vina said to Pike. "You don't need them."

"They may be just what I need," Pike said drily, beginning to recover some of his wits. "Number One, Yeoman, hand me those phasers."

They passed the weapons over. He examined them. What he found did not particularly surprise him. "Empty."

"They were fully charged when we left," Number One said.

"No doubt. But you'll find your communicators don't work either." A thought struck him. He looked quickly toward the almost circular panel he had found before. Then, suddenly, he hurled both phasers at it.

"What good does that do?" Number One said coolly.

"Don't talk to me. Don't say anything. I'm working up a hate—filling my mind with a picture of beating their huge, misshapen heads to a pulp. Thoughts so primitive they shut everything else out. I hate them—do you understand?"

"How long can you block your thoughts?" Vina said. "A few minutes, an hour? How can that help you?"

Pike concentrated, trying to pay no attention to her. She turned on the two other women.

"He doesn't need you," she said, with jealous anger she did not have to force-feed. "He's already picked me."

"Picked you for what?" Colt asked.

Vina looked at her scornfully. "Now there's a great chance for intelligent offspring."

" 'Offspring?' " Colt echoed. "As in 'children' "?

"As in he's 'Adam,' " Number One said, indicating Pike. "Isn't that it?"

"You're no better choice. They'd have better luck crossing him with a computer!"

"Shall I compute your age?" Number One said. "You were listed on that expedition as an adult crewman. Now, adding eighteen years to that . . ."

She broke off as Vina turned to the transparency. The Magistrate was back. The two crewwomen stared at him with interest.

"It's not fair," Vina said. "I did everything you asked."

The Magistrate ignored her. "Since you resist the present specimen," he said to Pike, "you now have a selection."

Pike threw himself at the impervious figure. "I'll break out, get to you somehow!" he shouted. "Is your blood red like ours? I'm going to find out!"

"Each of the two new specimens has qualities in her favor. The female you call 'Number One' has the superior mind and would produce highly intelligent offspring. Although she seems to lack emotion, this is largely a pretense. She often has fantasies involving you."

Number One looked flustered for the first time in Pike's memory, but he turned this, too, into rage at the invasion of her privacy. "All I want is to get my hands on you! Can you read these thoughts? Images of hate, killing . . ."

"The other new arrival has considered you unreachable, but is now realizing that this has changed. The factors in her favor are youth and strength, plus an unusually strong female emotion which . . ."

"You'll find my thoughts more interesting! Primitive thoughts you can't understand; emotions so ugly you can't . . ."

The pain hit him then and he went down, writhing. The images involved this time were from the torture chambers of the Inquisition. Over them, dimly, floated the Magistrate's thought, as though directed at someone else.

"Wrong thinking is punishable; right thinking will be as quickly rewarded. You will find it an effective combination."

The illusion vanished and Pike rolled weakly to a sitting position. He found the Magistrate gone, and the two crewwomen bending over him.

"No—don't—help me. Just leave me alone. Got to concentrate on hate. They can't read through it."

The hours wore on and eventually the lights went

down. It seemed obvious that the Talosians intended to keep all three women penned with him. Trying to keep the hate alive became increasingly more difficult; he slammed his fist against the enclosure wall again and again, hoping the pain would help.

The women conversed in low tones for a while, and then, one by one, fell asleep, Vina on the bed, the other two on the floor leaning against it. Pike squatted against the wall nearby, no thoughts in his mind now but roaring fatigue and the effort to fight it.

Then he sensed, rather than heard movement at his side. The wall panel had opened, and a Talosian arm was reaching in for the discarded phasers. He exploded into action, grabbing the arm and heaving.

The Magistrate was almost catapulted into the room by the force of that yank. Instantly, Pike's hands were around his throat.

"Don't hurt him!" Vina cried from the bed. "They don't mean to be evil . . ."

"I've had some samples of how 'good' they are . . ."

The Talosian vanished and Pike found himself holding the neck of the snarling anthropoid-spider creature he had first seen in a cell across from his. Its fangs snapped at his face. Colt shrieked.

Pike grimly tightened his grip. "I'm still holding your neck! Stop this illusion or I'll snap it!" The spider-thing changed back into the Magistrate again. "That's better. Try one more illusion—try anything at all—I'll take one quick twist. Understand?"

He loosened his hands slightly, allowing the Magistrate to gasp for breath. The forehead vein throbbed. "Your ship. Release me or we destroy it."

"He's not bluffing," Vina said. "With illusions they can make your crew work the wrong controls, push any button it takes to destroy the ship."

"I'll gamble he's too intelligent to kill for no reason at all. On the other hand, *I've* got a reason. Number One, take a good grip on his throat for me. And at the slightest excuse . . ."

"I understand, Captain," Number One said grimly.

Freed, Pike picked up the phasers. Putting one into

his belt, he adjusted the other, leveled it at the transparency, and pulled the trigger. As he expected, it didn't fire. He turned back to the Magistrate and pressed the weapon against his head.

"I'm betting," he said almost conversationally, "that you've created an illusion that this phaser is empty. That you don't know enough about your own machines, let alone ours, to dare to tamper with them. And that this one just blasted a hole in that wall which you're keeping us from seeing. Shall I test my theory on your head?"

The Magistrate closed his eyes resignedly. At once, there was a huge, jagged hole in the front of the cage.

"Q.E.D. Number One, you can let go of him now. If he acts up, I can shoot him, and he knows it. Everybody out. We're leaving!"

On the surface, only the top of the lift shaft still stood; the top of the knoll had been blasted clean off. So the Talosians had prevented the rescue party from seeing that, too.

Number One tried her communicator, but without effect. Noting the Magistrate's forehead vein throbbing again, Pike raised his phaser and said in a voice of iron, "I want contact with my ship. *Right now.*"

"No," said the Magistrate. "You are now on the surface where we intended you to be in the end. With the female of your choice, you will soon begin carefully guided lives . . ."

"Beginning with burying you."

"I see you intend to kill. I shall not prevent you; others of us will replace me. To help you reclaim the planet, our zoological gardens will furnish a variety of plant life . . ."

"Look," Pike said, "I'll make a deal with you. You and your life for the lives of these two Earthwomen."

"Since our life span is many times yours, we have time to evolve a society trained as artisans, technicans . . ."

"Do you understand what I'm saying? Give me proof our ship is all right, send these two back to it, and I'll stay here with Vina."

He felt a tug at his belt, and out of the corner of his eye saw that Number One had pulled the spare phaser out of it. The rachet popped like firecrackers as she turned the gain control full around. The phaser began to hum, rising in both pitch and volume. The weapon was building up an overload—a force chamber explosion.

"It's wrong," Number One said, "to create a whole race of humans to live as slaves. Do you concur, Captain?"

After a moment of hesitation, Pike nodded.

"Is this a deception?" asked the Magistrate. "Do you really intend to destroy yourselves? Yes, I see that you do."

"Vina, you've got time to get back underground. But hurry. And Talosian, to show just how primitive humans are, you can go with her."

The Magistrate did not move, nor did Vina.

"No," she said. "If you all think it's this important, then I can't leave either. I suppose if they still have one human, they might try again."

"We had not believed this possible," the Magistrate said, his thoughts betraying what might have been a strange sadness. "The customs and history of your race show a unique hatred of captivity, even when pleasant and benevolent. But you prefer death. This makes you too violent and dangerous a species for our needs."

"He means," Vina said, "they can't use you. You're free to go back to your ship."

Number One turned the phaser off, and just in time, too. In the renewed silence, Pike said, "Vina, that's it. No apologies. You captured one of us, threatened us, tortured us . . ."

"Your unsuitability has condemned the Talosian race to eventual death," the Magistrate said. "Is this not sufficient? No other specimens have shown your adaptability. You were our last hope."

"Nonsense," Pike said, surprised. "Surely some form of trade, some mutual cooperation . . ."

The Magistrate shook his head. "Your race would learn our power of illusion—and destroy itself. It is important to *our* beliefs to prevent this."

"Captain," Number One said, "we have Transporter control now."

"Good. Let's go. Vina, you too."

"I—" Vina said. "I can't go with you."

Pike felt a flash of what might almost have been exasperation. "Number One, Yeoman Colt, go aloft. I'll be with you when I've gotten to the bottom of this." As they hesitated, he added, "Orders."

They shimmered and vanished. Pike swung on Vina. "Now . . ."

He stopped, astounded and horrified. Vina was changing. Her face was wrinkling. An ugly scar appeared. Her body was becoming cruelly deformed. Throughout, she looked back at Pike with bitter eyes. The change did not stop until she was old, shockingly twisted, downright ugly.

"This is the female's true appearance," the Magistrate said.

It couldn't be true. *This* was the youngster of the survivors' camp, the sturdy peasant, the wife on Earth, the green Orionese savage who had danced so . . .

"This is the truth," Vina said, in an old woman's voice. She lifted her arms. "See me as I am. They found me in the wreckage, dying, nothing but a lump of flesh. They fixed me fine. Everything works. But—*they had no guide for putting me back together*.

"Do you understand now? Do you see why I can't go with you?"

She turned and stumbled toward the lift. Pike watched her go with horror and pity. Then he turned to the Magistrate, who said; "It was necessary to convince you that her desire to stay is an honest one."

Pike looked at him with new eyes. "You have some sparks of decency in you after all. Will you give her back her illusion of beauty?"

"We will. And more. See."

At the shaft, the image of the lovely Vina was entering the lift—*accompanied by himself*. The two turned and waved. Then the lift carried them down into the bowels of Talos IV.

"She has her illusion," the Magistrate said. Was he almost smiling? "And you have reality. May you find your way as pleasant."

Spock, Number One, Jose, Colt and Boyce all crowded toward him as he stepped out of the Transporter Chamber.

"What happened to Vina?" Colt demanded.

"Isn't she—coming with us?" asked Number One.

"No," Pike said shortly. "And I agree with her reasons. Now break it up here. What is this we're running, a cadet ship? Everybody on the bridge! Navigator, I want a course!"

"Yessir!"

They scattered like flushed partridges—all except Boyce, who said, "Hold on a minute, Captain."

"What for? I feel fine."

"That's the trouble. You look a hundred per cent better."

"I am. Didn't you recommend rest and change? I've had both. I've even been—home. Now, let's get on with things."

As the *Enterprise* moved away from Talos IV, routine re-established itself quickly, and the memory of all those illusions began to fade. They had not, after all, been real experiences—most of them. But Pike could not resist stealing a quick look from Number One to Colt, wondering which of them, in other circumstances, he might have picked.

When he found them both looking at him as if with the same speculation, he turned his eyes determinedly to the viewscreen and banished the thought.

He had had plenty of practice at that, lately.


## AFTERWORD

As the reader will now see, this story constituted the original pilot film for "Star Trek," and was shown as such at the 24th World Science Fiction Convention in Cleveland, Ohio, September 1—5, 1966. Between the selling of the series and the actual television broadcast of "The Menagerie," the whole concept of the cast changed radically. Number One was moved one step down in the chain of command, becoming Uhura, while her ostensible lack of emotion and computer-like mind were transferred to Spock; Yeoman Colt became Yeoman Rand;

Boyce became McCoy; Tyler became Sulu. The net effect was to make the new officers more interracial than before. The notion that the highly trained crew would ever be risked in ordinary hand-to-hand infantry combat was dropped.

Most important, perhaps, was that in the pilot film, Pike had wound up with a potentially explosive situation with two of his crewwomen which would be too complex to maintain through a long-term series of episodes. He had to be replaced, and the whole story turned into relatively ancient history; and thus was born Captain Kirk, and the framing story I have left out. All these stages are visible in the scripts I had to work from, which are heavily revised in various handwritings (and in which Pike confusingly appears from time to time as "Captain Spring" and "Captain Winter").

The only alternative would have been to reshoot the original "Menagerie" with the new cast, which would have been not only expensive, but would have produced all kinds of unwanted complexities in succeeding stories. Mr. Roddenberry obviously decided to let it stand as something that had happened way-back-when, and frame it as such. I think this was wise and I have followed his lead in this adaptation.

Ordinarily, writers should not inflict their technical problems on readers, who have every right to demand that such problems be solved before the story is published. But I sometimes get letters from "Star Trek" fans who castigate me for changing even one or two words in scripts they have memorized, or even have on tape. In this case, as in that of "The City on the Edge of Forever" (STAR TREK TWO), there were conflicts that couldn't be resolved by slavishly following the final text and ignoring how it had evolved. In both cases, I had to make my own judgment of what would best serve the authors' intents.

—J. B.

# THE ENTERPRISE INCIDENT

## (D. C. Fontana)

Operating under sealed orders, Kirk had found from long experience, almost always meant something messy. It became worse when the orders, once opened, demanded that they be kept secret from his own officers during the initial phases. And it was worst of all when those initial phases looked outright irrational.

Take the present situation. Here was the *Enterprise,* on the wrong side of the neutral zone, in Romulan space, surrounded by three Romulan cruisers which had simply popped out of nothingness, undetected by any sensor until far too late. Her presence there was a clear violation of a treaty; and since the Romulans were now using warships modeled on those of the Klingons, she was also heavily outgunned.

Kirk had worked out no way of making so suicidal a move on his part explicable except that of becoming irritable and snappish, as though his judgment had been worn down by fatigue. It was a bad solution. His officers were the best in Starfleet; sooner or later they would penetrate the deception, and conclude that whenever Kirk appeared to be worn down to the point of irrationality, he was operating under sealed orders.

And when the day came when he actually *was* too tired to know what he was doing, they would obey him blindly anyhow—and scratch one starship.

"Captain," Uhura said, her voice distant. "We are receiving a Class Two signal from one of the Romulan vessels."

"Put it on the main viewing screen, Lieutenant. Also, code a message to Starfleet Command, advising them of our situation and including all log entries to this point. Spock, your sensors read clear; what happened?"

"Sir, I have no more than a hypothesis . . ."

"Signal in," Uhura said. The main screen flickered briefly, then clarified to show a Romulan officer, with his own bridge behind him, carefully out of focus. He looked rather like Spock, and spoke like him, too.

"You have been identified as the Starship *Enterprise*. Captain James T. Kirk last known to be in command."

Kirk picked up a hand mike and thumbed its button. "Your information is correct. This is Captain Kirk."

"I am Subcommander Tal of the Romulan Imperial Fleet. Your ship is surrounded, Captain. You will surrender immediately—or we will destroy you."

Kirk flicked the switch and turned his face away toward Spock. He rather doubted that the Romulan could lip-read a foreign language, but there was no point in giving him the chance.

"Spock, come here. What do you make of this? They want something, or they would have destroyed us by now."

"No doubt, Captain. That would be standard procedure for them."

"It's my ship they want, I assume. And very badly."

"Of course. It would be a great prize. An elementary deduction, Captain."

"Skip the logic lessons." Kirk opened the mike again. "Save your threats, Subcommander," he said harshly. "If you attempt to board my ship, I'll blow her up. You gain nothing."

Tal had apparently expected nothing else, but a slight frown cut across his forehead nonetheless. "May I ask, Captain, who is that beside you?"

"My First Officer, Commander Spock. I'm surprised by your ignorance."

"You mean to insult me, but there is nothing discreditable in not knowing everything. Finding a Vulcan so highly placed in the Federation fleet does surprise me, I readily grant. However . . ."

He was interrupted by a beeping noise and hit an invisible control plate. "Yes, Commander? Excuse me, Captain . . ."

The screen dissolved into traveling moire patterns. Then Tal was back.

"No one should decide quickly to die, Captain," he said. "We give you one of your hours. If you do not surrender your ship at the end of that time, your destruction is certain. We will be open to communication, should you wish it."

"You understand Starfleet Command has been advised of our situation."

"Of course," Tal said, somewhat condescendingly. "But a subspace message will take three weeks to reach Starfleet—and I think they would hesitate to send a squadron in after you, in any event. The decision is yours, Captain. One hour."

His image winked out, and was replaced by stars.

"Lt. Uhura," Kirk said, "order all senior officers to report to the Briefing Room on the double."

"All right," Kirk said, surveying the group. Spock, McCoy and Scott were present; Chekov and Sulu on the bridge with Uhura. "Spock, you had a theory on why your sensors didn't pick up the Romulan ships, until they were right on top of us."

"I believe the Romulans have devised an improved cloaking system which renders our tracking sensors useless. You will observe, Captain, that the three ships outside are modeled after Klingon cruisers. Changing ship designs that drastically is expensive, and the Klingon cruiser has no important inherent advantages over the Romulan model of which we are aware—unless it is adaptable to some sort of novel screening device."

"If so, the Romulans could attack into Federation territory before we'd know they were there; before a planet or a vessel could begin to get its defenses up."

"They caught *us* right enough," Scott said.

"A brilliant observation, Mr. Scott," Kirk snapped. "Do you have any other helpful opinions?"

Scott was momentarily nonplussed. Then he pumped

his shoulders slightly in a shrug. "We've not got many choices . . ."

"Three. We can fight—and be destroyed. Or we can destroy the *Enterprise* ourselves to keep her from the Romulans. Or—we can surrender." There was a stir among the other officers; Kirk had expected it, and overrode it. "We might be able to find out how the Romulans' new cloaking device works. The Federation *must* have that information. Opinions?"

"Odds are against our finding out anything," Scott said. "And if the *Enterprise* is taken by the Romulans, they'll know everything there is to know about a starship."

"Spock?"

"If we had not crossed the Neutral Zone on your order," Spock said coldly and evenly, "you would not now require our opinions to bolster a decision that should never have had to be made."

The others stared at him, and then at Kirk. McCoy leaned forward. "Jim, *you* ordered us—? But you had no authority—"

"Dismissed, Doctor!"

"But Jim . . ."

"Bridge to Captain," Uhura's voice broke in.

"Kirk here."

"The Romulan vessel is signaling again, sir."

"Put it on our screen here, Lieutenant."

The triangular Briefing Room viewscreen lit up to show the Vulcan-like features of Tal. He said without preamble, "My Commander wishes to speak with you, Captain Kirk."

"Very well," Kirk said, slightly surprised. "Put him on."

"The Commander wishes to see you and your First Officer aboard this vessel. It is felt that the matter requires—discussion. The Commander is a highly placed representative of the Romulan Star Empire."

"Why should we walk right into your hands?"

"Two of my officers will beam aboard your vessel as exchange hostages while you are here."

"There's no guarantee they'll transport over here once we've entered your ship."

A faint, cynical smile seemed to be threatening to break over Tal's face. "Granted we do not easily trust each other, Captain. But *you* are the ones who violated our territory. Should it not be we who distrust *your* motives? However, we will agree to a simultaneous exchange."

Perfect—and yet at the same time, impossible to explain to his worriedly watching officers. After appearing to consider, Kirk said, "Give us the transporter coordinates and synchronize."

Tal nodded and his image faded.

"I must insist on advising against this, Captain," protested Scott. "The Romulans will try something tricky . . ."

"We'll learn nothing by staying aboard the *Enterprise*," Kirk said. "One final order. Engineer Scott, you are in charge. If we do not return, this ship must not be taken. If the Romulans attempt it, you will fight—and if necessary, destroy the *Enterprise*. Is that clear?"

"Perfectly, Captain." In point of fact, Scott looked as though it was the first order he had understood in days. Well, with any luck, he'd understand all the rest later— if there was going to be any "later."

"Very well. Alert Transporter Officer."

Kirk and Spock were conducted to the quarters of the Romulan Commander by two guards, after having been relieved of their weapons. Had the necessity existed, those two guards would never have known what had hit them, sidearms or no, but nothing was to be gained now by overpowering them; Kirk merely noted the overconfidence for possible future use.

Then the door snapped open—and the Romulan Commander, standing behind a desk, was revealed to be a woman. And no ordinary woman, either. Of course, no ordinary woman could become both a ranking officer and a government representative in a society of warriors; but this one was beautiful, aristocratic, compelling—an effect which was, if anything, heightened by the fact that she was of Vulcanoid, not human stock. Kirk and Spock looked quickly at each other. Kirk had the impression that if Spock could whistle, he would.

"Captain Kirk," she said.

"I'm honored, Commander."

"I do not think so, Captain. But we have a matter of importance to discuss, and your superficial courtesies are the overture to that discussion." Her eyes swung leveling to Spock. "You are First Officer . . .?"

"Spock."

"I speak first with the Captain."

Spock flicked a glance at Kirk, who nodded. The First Officer tilted a half bow toward the Commander, and Kirk entered the office. The door snapped shut behind him.

"All right," he said. "Forgetting the superficial courtesies, let's just have at it. I'm not surrendering my ship to you."

"An admirable attitude in a starship captain," she said coolly. "But the matter of trespass into Romulan space is one of galactic import—a violation of treaties. Now I ask you simply: what is your mission here?"

"Instrument failure caused a navigational error. We were across the Zone before we realized it. Your ships surrounded us before we could turn about."

"A starship—one of Starfleet's finest vessels. You are saying instrument failure as radical as you suggest went unnoticed until your ship was well past the Neutral Zone?"

"Accidents happen; cutoffs and backup systems can malfunction. We've been due in for overhaul for two months, but haven't been assigned a space dock yet."

"I see. But you have managed to navigate with this malfunction?"

"The error has been corrected," Kirk said. He knew well enough how transparent the lie was, but the charade had to be played out; he needed to seem thoroughly outgunned—in all departments.

"Most convenient. I hardly believe it will clear you of espionage."

"We were not spying."

"Your language has always been difficult for me, Captain," the woman said drily. "Perhaps you have another word for it?"

"At worst, it would be nothing more than surveillance. But I assure you that you are drawing an unjustified . . ."

"Captain, if a Romulan vessel ventured far into Federation territory without good explanation, what would a Star Base commander do? It works both ways—and I strongly doubt you are the injured party." She pressed a button and the door opened. "Spock, come in. Both the Federation Council and the Romulan Praetor are being informed of this situation, but the time will be long before we receive their answer. I wish to interrogate you to establish a record of information for them in the meantime. The Captain has already made his statement."

"I understand," Spock said.

"I admit to some surprise on seeing you, Spock. We were not aware of Vulcans aboard the *Enterprise*."

"Starfleet is not in the habit of informing Romulans of its ships' personnel."

"Quite true. Yet certain ships—certain officers—are known to us. Your situation appears most interesting."

"What earns Spock your special interest?" Kirk broke in.

"His species, obviously. Our forebears had the same roots and origins—something you will never understand, Captain. We can appreciate the Vulcans—our distant brothers. Spock, I have heard of Vulcan integrity and personal honor. There is a well-known saying that Vulcans are incapable of lying. Or is it a myth?"

"It is no myth."

"Then tell me truthfully now: on your honor as a Vulcan, what was your mission?"

"I reserve the privilege of speaking the truth only when it will not violate my honor as a Vulcan."

"It is unworthy of a Vulcan to resort to subterfuge."

"It is equally unworthy of a Romulan," Spock said. "It is not a lie to keep the truth to one's self."

That was one sentence too many, Kirk thought. But given Spock's nature and role, it could hardly have been prevented. The woman was wily as well as intelligent.

"Then," she said, "there is a truth here that is still unspoken."

"You have been told everything that there is to know," Kirk said. "There is nothing else."

"There is Mr. Spock's unspoken truth. You knew of the cloaking device that we have developed. You deliberately violated Romulan space in a blatant spy mission on the order of Federation Command."

"We've been through that, Commander."

"We have not even begun, Captain. There is of course no force I can use on a Vulcan that will make him speak. But there are Romulan methods capable of going into a human mind like a spike into a melon. We use them when the situation requires it."

"Then you know," Spock said, "that they are ineffective against humans with Command training."

"Of course," said the Commander. "They will leave him dead—or what might be worse than dead. But I would be replaced did I not apply them as Procedure dictates. One way or another, I will know your unspoken truths."

To Kirk, Spock's iron expression never seemed to change, but now he caught a very faint flicker of indecision which must have spoken volumes to the Romulan woman. Kirk said hastily, "Let her rant. There is nothing to say."

Spock did not look at him. "I cannot allow the Captain to be any further destroyed," the First Officer said in a low monotone. "The strain of command has worn heavily on him. He has not been himself for several weeks."

"There's a lie," Kirk said, "if ever I heard one."

"As you can see," Spock continued evenly, "Captain Kirk is a highly sensitive and emotional person. I believe he has lost his capacity for rational decision."

"Shut up, Spock."

"I am betraying no secrets. The Commander's suspicion that Starfleet ordered the *Enterprise* into the Zone is unacceptable. Our rapid capture demonstrates its foolhardiness."

"Spock—damn you, what are doing?"

"I am speaking the truth for the benefit of the *Enter-*

102

*prise* and the Federation. I say—for the record—that Captain Kirk took the *Enterprise* across the Neutral Zone on his own initiative and his craving for glory. He is not sane."

"And I say," Kirk returned between tightly drawn lips, "that you are a filthy traitor."

"Enough," the Commander said, touching a control plate on her desk. "Give me communication with the *Enterprise*."

After a long moment, Scott's voice said, *"Enterprise;* Acting Officer Scott."

"Officer Scott, Captain James T. Kirk is formally charged with espionage. The testimony of First Officer Spock has confirmed that this intrusion into Romulan space was not an accident; and that your ship was not under orders from Starfleet Command or the Federation Council to undertake such a mission. Captain Kirk was solely responsible. Since the crew had no choice but to obey orders, the crew will not be held responsible. Therefore I am ordering Engineer Scott, presently in command of the *Enterprise,* to follow the Romulan flagship to our home base. You will there be processed and released to Federation Command. Until judgment is passed, Captain Kirk will be held in confinement."

There were a few moments of dead air from the *Enterprise,* but Kirk had no difficulty in guessing what Scotty was doing: ordering the two Romulan hostages to be put in the brig. When he came on again, his voice was almost shaking with suppressed rage.

"This is Lt. Commander Scott. The *Enterprise* follows no orders except those of Captain Kirk. We will stay right here until he returns. And if you make any attempt to commandeer or board us, the *Enterprise* will be blown to bits along with as many of you as we can take with us. Your own knowledge of our armament will tell you that that will be quite a good many."

"You humans make a very brave noise," the Commander said. She sounded angry herself, although her face was controlled. "There are ways to convince you of your errors."

103

She cut off communication with a flick of a switch. Kirk swung on Spock.

"Did you hear, you pointy-eared turncoat? You've betrayed everything of value and integrity you ever knew. Did you hear the sound of human integrity?"

"Take him to the Security Room."

The guards dragged Kirk out.


"'It was your testimony that Captain Kirk was irrational and solely responsible that saved the lives of your crew," the Romulan Commander said. "But don't expect gratitude for it."

"One does not expect logic from humans," Spock said. "As we both know."

"A Vulcan among humans—living, working with them. I would think the situation would be intolerable to you."

"I am half Vulcan. My mother was human."

"To whom is your allegiance, then?" she asked with cool interest. "Do you call yourself Terran or Vulcan?"

"Vulcan."

"How long have you been a Starfleet officer, Spock?"

"Eighteen years."

"You serve Captain Kirk. Do you like him? Do you like your shipmates?"

"The question is irrelevant."

"Perhaps." She drew closer, looking into his eyes challengingly. "But you are subordinate to the Captain's orders. Even to his whims."

"My duty as an officer," Spock said rigidly, "is to obey him."

"You are a superior being. Why do you not command?"

Spock hesitated. "I do not desire a ship of my own."

"Of course you believe that now, after eighteen years. But is it not also true that no one has given you—a Vulcan—that opportunity?"

"Such opportunities are extremely rare."

"For one of your accomplishments and—capabilities— opportunities should be made. And will be. I can see to that—if you will stop looking at the Federation as the whole universe. It is not, you know."

"The thought has occasionally crossed my mind," Spock said.

"You must have your own ship."

"Commander," Spock said pleasantly, "shall we speak plainly? It is you who desperately need a ship. You want the *Enterprise*."

"Of course! It would be a great triumph for me to bring the *Enterprise* home intact. It would broaden the scope of my powers greatly. It would be the achievement of a lifetime." She paused. "And naturally, it would open equal opportunities to you."

The sound of an intercom spared Spock the need to reply. It was not an open line; the Commander picked up a handset and listened. After a moment she said, "I will come there," and replaced it. Spock raised his eyebrows inquiringly.

"Your Captain," she said with a trace of scorn, "tried to break through the sonic disruptor field which wards his cell. Naturally he is injured, and since we do not know how to treat humans, my First Officer asked your ship's surgeon to attend him. The man's first response was, 'I don't make house calls,' whatever that means, but we managed to convince him that it was not a trick and he is now in attendance. Follow me, please."

She led the way out of the office and down the corridor, followed by the omnipresent, silent guards.

"I neglected to mention it," she added, "but I will expect you for dinner. We have much yet to discuss."

"Indeed?" Spock said, looking at her quizzically.

"Allow me to rephrase. Will you join me for dinner?"

"I am honored, Commander. Are the guards also invited?"

For answer, she waved the guards off. They seemed astonished, but were soon out of sight. A moment later she and Spock reached a junction; to the left, the corridor continued, while to the right it brought up against a single door not far away; it was guarded. There was a raised emblem nearby, but from this angle Spock could not read the device on it. He moved toward it.

"Mr. Spock!"

He stopped instantly.

"That corridor is forbidden to all but loyal Romulans."

"Of course, Commander," Spock said. "I will obey your restrictions."

"I hope," she said, "soon there will be no need for you to observe *any* restrictions."

"It would be illogical to assume that all conditions remain stable."

They reached the Romulan brig; a guard there saluted and turned off the disruptor field. When they entered the cell, he turned it on again. McCoy was there—and so was Kirk, sitting slumped and blank-eyed on the bed, hands hanging down loosely between his knees.

"You are the physician?" the Commander said.

"McCoy—Chief Medical Officer."

"Captain Kirk's condition?"

"Physically—weak. Mentally—depressed, disoriented, displays feelings of persecution and rebellion."

"Then by your own standards of normality, this man is not fully competent?"

"Not now," McCoy said reluctantly. "No."

"Mr. Spock has stated he believes the Captain had no authority or order to cross the Neutral Zone. In your opinion, could this mental incapacity have afflicted the Captain earlier?"

"Yes—it's possible."

"Mr. Spock, the Doctor has now confirmed your testimony as to the mental state of your Captain. He was and is unfit to continue in command of the *Enterprise*. That duty has now fallen upon you. Are you ready to exercise that function?"

"I am ready."

McCoy looked aghast. "Spock—I don't believe it!"

"The matter," Spock said, "is not open for discussion."

"What do you mean, not open for discussion? If . . ."

"That's enough, Doctor," the Commander broke in. "As a physician, your duty is to save lives. Mr. Spock's duty is to lead the *Enterprise* to a safe haven."

"There is no alternative, Doctor," Spock added. "The safety of the crew is the paramount issue. It is misguided loyalty to resist any further."

Kirk raised his head very slowly. He looked a good

deal more than disoriented; he looked downright mad. Then, suddenly, he was lunging at Spock, his voice a raw scream:

"Traitor! I'll—kill—you!"

With the swift precision of a surgeon, Spock grasped Kirk's shoulder and the back of his neck in both hands. The raging Captain stiffened, cried out inarticulately once, and collapsed.

Spock looked down at him, frozen. The guard had drawn his sidearm. McCoy kneeled beside the crumpled Captain, snapped out an instrument, took a reading, prepared a hypo in desperate haste.

"What did you do to him?" McCoy demanded. He administered the shot and then looked up. His voice became hard, snarling. *"What did you do?"*

"I was unprepared for his attack," Spock said. "He—I used the Vulcan death grip instinctively."

McCoy tried a second shot, then attempted to find a pulse or heartbeat.

"Your instincts are still good, Spock," he said with cold remoteness. "He's dead."

"By his own folly," said the Romulan Commander. "Return the corpse and the Doctor to their vessel. Mr. Spock, shall we proceed to dinner?"

"That," Spock said, "sounds rather more pleasant."

It was pleasant indeed; it had been a long time since Spock had seen so sumptuously laden a table. He poured more wine for the Commander.

"I have had special Vulcan dishes prepared for you," she said. "Do they meet with your approval?"

"I am flattered, Commander. There is no doubt that the cuisine aboard your vessel far surpasses that of the *Enterprise*. It is indeed a powerful recruiting inducement."

"We have other inducements." She arose and came over to sit down beside him. "You have nothing in Starfleet to which to return. I—*we* offer an alternative. We will find a place for you, if you wish it."

"A—place?"

"With me." She touched his sleeve, his shoulder, then his neck, brushing lightly. "Romulan women are not like

Vulcan females. We are not dedicated to pure logic and the sterility of non-emotion. Our people are warriors, often savage; but we are also many other—pleasant things."

"I was not aware of that aspect of Romulan society."

"As a Vulcan, you would study it," she said softly. "But as a human, you would find ways to appreciate it."

"You must believe me, I do appreciate it."

"I'm so glad. There is one final step to make the occasion complete. You will lead a small party of Romulans aboard the *Enterprise*. You will take your rightful place as its commander and lead the ship to a Romulan port —with my flagship at its side."

"Yes, of course," Spock said impatiently. "But not just this minute, surely. An hour from now will do—even better. Will it not, Commander?"

She actually laughed. "Yes, it will, Mr. Spock. And you do know that I have a first name."

"I was beginning to wonder."

She leaned forward and whispered. The word would have meant absolutely nothing to a human, but Spock recognized its roots without difficulty.

"How rare and how beautiful," he said. "But so incongruous when spoken by a soldier."

"If you will give me a moment, the soldier will transform herself into a woman." She rose, and he rose with her. Her hand trailed out of his, and a door closed behind her.

Spock turned his back to it, reached inside his tunic, and brought out his communicator. Snapping it open, he said quietly, "Spock to Captain Kirk."

"Kirk here. I'm already on board—green skin, pointed ears, uniform and all. Do you have the information?"

"Yes, the device is down the first corridor to the left as you approach the Commander's office, closely guarded and off limits to all but authorized personnel."

"I'll get it. Will you be able to get back to the *Enterprise* without attracting their attention?"

"Unknown. At present . . ."

"Somebody coming. Out."

Spock replaced the communicator quickly, but it was a long minute before the Commander returned. The change was quite startling; compared to her appearance in uniform, she seemed now to be wearing hardly anything, although this was in part an illusion of contrast.

"Mr. Spock?" she said, posing. "Is my attire now more —appropriate?"

"More than that. It should actually stimulate our conversation."

She raised her hand, fingers parted in the Vulcan manner, and he followed suit. They touched each other's faces.

"It's hard to believe," she said, "that I could be so stirred by the touch of an alien hand."

"I too—must confess—that I am moved emotionally. I know it is illogical—but . . ."

"Spock, we need not question what we truly feel. Accept what is happening between us, even as I do."

"I question no further."

"Come, then." Taking his hand, she turned toward the other room.

The outside door buzzed stridently. Had Spock been fully human, he would have jumped.

"Commander!" Tal's voice called. "Permission to enter!"

"Not now, Tal."

"It is urgent, Commander."

She hesitated, looking at Spock, but her mood had been broken. She said; "Very well—you may enter."

There were two guards behind Tal. It would have been hard to say whether they were more surprised by Spock's presence or by their Commander's state of undress, but discipline reasserted itself almost at once.

"Commander. We have intercepted an alien transmission from aboard our own vessel."

"Triangulate and report."

"We have already done so, Commander. The source is in this room."

She stiffened and turned to Spock. Gazing levelly at her, he reached under his tunic. Tal and the guards drew their weapons. Moving very slowly, Spock brought out his communicator and proffered it to her. Trancelike,

109

without looking away from his face, she took the device. Then, suddenly, she seemed to awaken.

"The cloaking device! Send guards . . ."

"We thought of that also, Commander," Tal said. The slight stress on her title dripped with contempt. It was clear that he thought it would shortly pass to him. "It is gone."

"Full alert. Search all decks."

"That will be profitless, Commander," Spock said. "I do not believe you will find it."

Her response was a cry of shock. "You must be mad!"

"I assure you, I am quite sane."

"Why would you do this to me? What are you that you could do this?"

"I am," Spock said, not without some regret, "the First Officer of the *Enterprise*."

She struck him, full in the face. Nobody could have mistaken it for a caress. The blow would have dropped any human being like a felled ox.

He merely looked at her, his face calm. She glared back, and gradually her breathing became more even.

"Take him to my office. I shall join you shortly."

She was back in uniform now, and absolutely expressionless. "Execution for state criminals," she said, "is both painful and demeaning. I believe the details are unnecessary. The sentence will be carried out immediately after charges are recorded."

"I am not a Romulan subject," Spock said. "But if I am to be treated as one, I demand the Right of Statement first."

"So you know more about Romulan custom than you let appear. This increases your culpability. However, the right is granted."

"Thank you."

"Return to your station, Subcommander," she said to Tal. "The boarding action will begin on my order."

Tal saluted and left. The Commander took a weapon from her desk, and laid it before her. She seemed otherwise confident that Spock would make no ignominious attempts at escape; and indeed, even had the situation been

110

as she thought, such an attempt would have been illogical.

"There is no time limit to the Right of Statement, but I will not appreciate many hours of listening to your defense."

"I will not require much time," Spock said. "No more than twenty minutes, I would say."

"It should take less time than that to find your ally who stole the cloaking device. You will not die alone." She tapped a button on the desk console. "Recording. The Romulan Right of Statement allows the condemned to make a statement of official record in defense or explanation of his crime. Commander Spock, Starfleet Officer and proven double agent, demands the right. Proceed, Commander Spock."

"My crimes are espionage, and aiding and abetting sabotage. To both of these I freely admit my guilt. However, Lords Praetori, I reject the charge of double agentry, with its further implication of treason. However I may have attempted to make the matter appear, and regardless of my degree of success in such a deception, I never at any point renounced my loyalty to the Federation, let alone swearing allegiance to the Romulan Empire.

"I was in fact acting throughout under sealed orders from Starfleet Command, whose nature was unknown to anyone aboard the *Enterprise* except, of course, Captain Kirk. These orders were to find out whether the Romulans had in fact developed a rumored cloaking device for their ships, and if so, to obtain it by any possible means. The means actually employed were worked out in secret by Captain Kirk and myself."

"And so," the Commander said with bitter contempt, "the story that Vulcans cannot lie is a myth after all."

"Of course, Commander. Complex interpersonal relationships among sentient beings absolutely require a certain amount of lying, for the protection of others and the good of the whole. Among humans such untruths are called 'white lies.' A man's honor in this area is measured by whether he can tell the difference between a white lie and a malicious one. It is a much more delicate matter than simply charging blindly ahead telling the truth at all

111

times, no matter what injury the truth may sometimes do. And there are occasions, such as the present one, when one must weigh a lie which will cause personal injury against a truth which would endanger the good of the whole. Your attempt to seduce and subvert me, Commander, was originally just that kind of choice. If it became something else, I am sorry, but such a danger is always present in such attempts."

"I can do without your pity," the Commander said, "and your little moral lecture. Pray proceed."

"As you wish. The oath I swore as a Starfleet officer is both explicit and binding. So long as I wear the uniform it is my duty to protect the security of the Federation. Clearly, your new cloaking device presents a threat to that security. I carried out my duty as my orders and my oath required."

"Everyone carries out his duty, Mr. Spock," the Commander said. "You state the obvious."

"There is no regulation concerning the content of the statement. May I continue?"

"Very well. Your twenty minutes are almost up."

"I trust that the time consumed by your interruptions and my answers to them will not be charged against me. Interrogation in the midst of a formal Statement is most irregular."

The Commander threw up her hands. "These endless quibbles! Will you kindly get back to the point?"

"Certainly. The Commander's appeal to my Vulcan loyalties, in the name of our remote common racial origin, was bound to fail; since beyond the historic tradition of Vulcan loyalty there is the combined Vulcan/Romulan history of obedience to duty—and Vulcan is, may I remind you, a member of the United Federation of Planets. In other words . . ."

Under his voice, a familiar hum began to grow in the room. The Commander realized instantly what was happening—but instead of picking up the sidearm and firing, as she had plenty of time to do despite all Spock's droning attempt to dull her attention—she sprang forward and threw her arms around him. Then both were frozen in a torrent of sparks . . .

And both were in the Transporter Room of the *Enterprise*.

As the elevator doors opened onto the bridge, Kirk's voice boomed out.

"Throw the switch on that device, Scotty!"

"I did, sir," Scott's voice said. "It's not working."

The Commander looked in Kirk's direction and a muffled exclamation escaped her as Spock escorted her out. Kirk had not yet removed his Romulan Centurion's uniform, let alone bothered to change his skin color or have his surgically altered ears restored to normal human shape. Obviously, the other half of the plot was now all too clear to her.

Spock left her and crossed to his station. Behind him, her voice said steadily, "I would give you credit, Captain, for getting this far—but you will be dead in a moment and the credit would be gratuitous."

The Captain ignored her. "Lt. Uhura, open a channel to the Romulan command vessel; two-way visual contact."

"Right . . . I have Subcommander Tal, sir."

Tal seemed quite taken aback to see what appeared to be one of his own officers in the command chair, but must have realized in the next second that any Centurion he did not recognize had to be an imposter. He said almost instantly, "We have you under our main batteries, *Enterprise*. You cannot escape."

"This is Captain Kirk under this silly outfit. Hold your fire. We have your Commander with us."

Tal shot a look toward where his own main viewscreen evidently was located. "Commander!"

"Subcommander Tal," the woman said, "I am giving you a direct order. Obey it. *Close and destroy!*"

Uhura cut off transmission, but not fast enough. It was a risk that had had to be taken.

"Come on, Scotty, we've run out of time."

"Captain, I'm working as fast as I can."

"You see, Captain," the Commander said, "your effort is wasted."

"Mr. Spock. Distance from the Romulan vessels."

113

"One hundred fifty thousand kilometers and closing rapidly."

"Stand to phasers. You'll forgive me if I put up a fight, Commander."

"Of course," the woman said. "That is expected."

"One hundred thousand kilometers," Spock said. "They'll be within maximum range within six seconds . . . five . . . four . . ."

"Scott, *throw the switch!*"

"It'll likely overload, but . . ."

". . . two . . . one . . ."

"Functioning, Captain!"

"Mr. Chekov, change course to 318 mark 7, Warp Nine."

"Nine, sir? . . . Done."

Spock turned toward Kirk. "They have opened fire at where we were last, sir, but the cloaking device appears to be operating most effectively. And the Commander informed me that even their own sensors cannot track a vessel so equipped."

"Thank you, Mr. Spock," Kirk said in a heartfelt voice. He turned to the Commander. "We will leave you at a Federation outpost."

"You are most gracious, Captain. If I may be taken to your brig, I will take my place as your prisoner. Further attendance here is painful to me."

Kirk stood, very formal. "Mr. Spock, the honor of escorting the Commander to her *quarters* is yours."

The two opposing forces bowed formally to each other, and Spock led the Commander back toward the elevator. Behind them, Sulu's voice said, "Entering Neutral Zone, Captain."

"I'm sorry you were made an unwilling passenger," Spock said. "It was not intentional. All they really wanted was the cloaking device."

"They? And what did you want?"

"That is all I wanted when I went aboard your vessel."

"And that is exactly all you came away with."

"You underestimate yourself, Commander."

She refused to hear the hidden meaning. "You realize

114

that we will very soon learn to penetrate the cloaking device. After all, we discovered it; you only stole it."

"Obviously, military secrets are the most fleeting of all," he said. "I hope we exchange something more permanent."

She stepped into the elevator; but when Spock tried to follow her, she barred the way. "You made the choice."

"It was the only choice possible. Surely you would not have respected any other."

She looked at him for a long moment, and then smiled, slightly, sadly. "That will be our—secret. Get back to your duty. The guards had best take me from here."

Spock beckoned to two guards. She could probably incapacitate both in a matter of seconds, but they were well out of Transporter range of any of the Romulan ships now—and her mood did not seem to be one which would impel her to illogical action. In a way it was a pity that she obviously did not know that Vulcans were cyclical in their mating customs, and immune to sexual attraction at all other times. Or had she been counting on his human side? And—had she been right to do so?

The elevator swallowed her down. Spock went back to his post.

"Sickbay to Captain Kirk. If all the shouting's over up there, I want you to report to me."

"What for, Bones?"

"You're due in surgery again. As payment for the big act of irrationality you put over on me, I'm going to bob your ears."

Kirk grinned and touched the ears, which apparently he had forgotten in the heat of operations, and looked over at Spock.

"Please go, Captain," Spock said in a remote voice. "Somehow, they are not aesthetically pleasing on a human."

"Are you coming, Jim?" McCoy's voice said. "Or do you want to go through the rest of your life looking like your First Officer?"

And McCoy had the last word again.

# A PIECE OF THE ACTION

## (David P. Harmon and Gene L. Coon)

It was difficult to explain to Bela Okmyx, who called himself "Boss" of Dana Iotia Two, that though the message from the lost *Horizon* had been sent a hundred years ago, the *Enterprise* had only received it last month. For that matter, he did not seem to know what the "galaxy" meant, either.

Kirk did not know what he expected to find, but he was braced for anything. Subspace radio was not the only thing the *Horizon* had lacked. She had landed before the non-interference directive had come into effect, and while the Iotians were just at the beginnings of industrialization. And the Iotians had been reported to be extremely intelligent—and somewhat imitative. The *Horizon* might have changed their culture drastically before her departure and shipwreck.

Still, the man called Boss seemed friendly enough. He didn't understand what "transported" meant either, in the technical sense, but readily suggested a rendezvous at an intersection marked by a big building with white columns in a public square where, he said, he would provide a reception committee. All quite standard, so far.

Kirk, Spock and McCoy beamed down, leaving Scott at the con. They materialized into a scene which might at first have been taken for an area in any of the older cities of present-day Earth, but with two significant exceptions; no children were visible, and all the adults, male and female alike, were wearing sidearms. Their dress was reminiscent of the United States of the early twentieth century.

This had barely registered when a sharp male voice

behind them said, "Okay, you three. Let's see you petrify."

The officers turned to find themselves confronted by two men carrying clumsy two-handed weapons which Kirk recognized as a variant of the old submachine gun.

"Would you mind clarifying your statement, please?" Spock said.

"I want to see you turn to stone. Put your hands up over your head—or you ain't gonna have no head to put your hands over."

The two were standing close enough together so that Kirk could have stunned them both from the hip, but he disliked stopping situations before they had even begun to develop. He obeyed, his officers following suit.

The man who had spoken kept them covered while the other silently relieved them of their phasers and communicators. He seemed momentarily in doubt about McCoy's tricorder, but he took that, too. A few pedestrians stopped to watch; they seemed only mildly curious, and some of them even seemed to approve. Were these men policemen, then? They were dressed no differently from anyone else; perhaps more expensively and with more color, but that was all.

The silent man displayed his harvest to his spokesman. The latter took a phaser and examined it. "What's this?"

"Be very careful with that, please," Kirk said. "It's a weapon."

"A heater, huh? The Boss'll love that."

"A Mr. Bela Okmyx invited us down. He said . . ."

"I know what he said. What he don't tell Kalo ain't worth knowing. He said some boys would meet you. Okay, we're meeting you."

"Those guns aren't necessary," McCoy said.

"You trying to make trouble, bud? Don't give me those baby blue eyes."

"What?"

"I don't buy that innocent routine." Kalo looked at Spock's ears. "You a boxer?"

"No," Spock said. "Why does everybody carry firearms? Are you people at war?"

"I never heard such stupid questions in my life." Kalo jerked his gun muzzle down the street. "Get moving."

118

As they began to walk, Kirk became aware of a distant but growing thrumming sound. Suddenly a squeal was added to it and it became much larger.

"Get down!" Kalo shouted, throwing himself to the street. The people around him were already dropping, or seeking shelter. Kirk dived for the dirt.

A vehicle that looked like two mismatched black bricks on four wheels bore down on them. Two men leaned out of it with submachine guns, which suddenly produced a terrible, hammering roar. Kalo got off a burst at it, but his angle was bad for accuracy. Luckily, it was not good for the gunners in the car, either.

Then the machine was gone, and the pedestrians picked themselves up. McCoy looked about, then knelt by the silent member of the "reception committee," but he was plainly too late.

Kalo shook his head. "Krako's getting more gall all the time."

"Is this the way you greet all your visitors?" Kirk demanded.

"It happens, pal."

"But this man is dead," McCoy said.

"Yeah? Well, we ain't playing for peanuts. Hey, you dopes, get outta here!" He shouted suddenly to what looked like the beginning of a crowd. "Ain't you never seen a hit before? Get lost!"

He resumed herding his charges, leaving the dead man unconcernedly behind. Kirk kept his face impassive, but his mind was busy. A man had been shot down, and no one had blinked an eye; it seemed as though it were an everyday happening. Was this the cultural contamination they had been looking for? But the crew of the *Horizon* hadn't been made up of cold-blooded killers, nor had they reported the Iotian culture in that state.

A young girl, rather pretty, emerged from a store entrance and cut directly across to them, followed by another. "You, Kalo," she said.

"Get lost."

"When's the Boss going to do something about the crummy street lights around here? A girl ain't safe."

"And how about the laundry pickup?" said the second girl. "We ain't had a truck by in three weeks."

"Write him a letter," Kalo said indifferently.

"I did. He sent it back with postage due."

"Listen, we pay our percentages. We're entitled to some service for our money."

"Get *lost,* I said." Kalo shook his head as the girls sullenly fell behind. "Some people got nothing to do but complain."

Kirk stared at him. He was certainly an odd sight—odder than before, now that his pockets were stuffed with all the hand equipment from the *Enterprise* trio, and he had a submachine gun under each arm. But he looked none the less dangerous for that. "Mr. Kalo, is this the way your citizens get things done? Their right of petition?"

"If they pay their percentages, the Boss takes care of them. We go in here."

"In here" was a building bearing a brightly polished brass plaque. It read:

### BELA OKMYX
#### BOSS
#### NORTHSIDE TERRITORY

The end of the line was an office, large and luxurious, complete with heavy desk, a secretary of sorts and framed pictures—except that one of the frames, Kirk saw, surrounded some kind of pistol instead. A heavy-set, swarthy man sat behind the desk.

"Got 'em, Boss," Kalo said. "No sweat."

The big man smiled and rose. "Well, Captain Kirk. Come in. Sit down. Have a drink. Good stuff—distill it myself."

"No, thank you. You are Mr. Okmyx? This is Mr. Spock, my First Officer. And Dr. McCoy."

"A real pleasure. Sit down. Put down the heater, Kalo. These guys is guests." He turned back to Kirk. "You gotta excuse my boys. You just gotta be careful these days."

"Judging from what we've seen so far, I agree." Kirk said. "They call you the Boss. Boss of what?"

"My territory. Biggest in the world. Trouble with being the biggest is that punks is alla time trying to cut in."

"There is something astonishingly familiar about all this, Captain," Spock said.

"How many other territories are there?"

"Maybe a dozen, not counting the small fry—and they get bumped anyway when I get around to it."

"Do they include, if I may ask," Spock said, "a gentleman named Krako?"

"You know about Krako?"

"He hit us, Boss," Kalo said. "Burned Mirt."

Bela scowled. "I want him hit back."

"I'll take care of it."

Kirk had noticed a huge book on a stand nearby. He rose and moved toward it. Kalo raised his gun muzzle again, but at a quick signal from Bela, dropped it. The book was bound like a Bible, in white leather, with gold lettering reading: *Chicago Mobs of the Twenties*. The imprint was New York, 1993.

"How'd you get this, Mr. Okmyx?" he asked.

"That's The Book. *The* Book. They left it—the men from the *Horizon*."

"And there is your contamination, Captain," Spock said. "An entire gangster culture. An imitative people, one book, and . . ."

"No cracks about The Book," Bela said harshly. "Look, I didn't bring you here for you to ask questions. You gotta do something for me. Then I tell you anything you want to know."

"Anything we can do," Kirk said, putting the book down, "we will. We have laws of our own we must observe."

"Okay," Bela said. He leaned forward earnestly. "Look, I'm a peaceful man, see? I'm sick and tired of all the hits. Krako hits me, I hit Krako, Tepo hits me, Krako hits Tepo. We ain't getting noplace. There's too many bosses, know what I mean? Now if there was just one, maybe we could get some things done. That's where you come in."

"I don't quite understand," Kirk said.

"You Feds made a lot of improvements since the other

121

ship came here. You probably got all kinds of fancy heaters. So here's the deal. You gimme all the heaters I need—enough tools so I can hit all the punks once and for all—and I take over the whole place. Then all you have to deal with is me."

"Let me get this straight," Kirk said. "You want us to supply you with arms and assistance so you can carry out aggression against other nations?"

"What nations? I got some hits to make. You help me make them."

"Fascinating," Spock said. "But quite impossible."

"I'd call it outrageous," McCoy said.

"Even if we wanted to," Kirk said, "our orders are very . . ."

Bela gestured to Kalo, who raised his gun again. Though Kirk did not see any signal given, the door opened and another armed man came in.

"I ain't interested in *your* orders," Bela said. "You got eight hours to gimme what I asked for. If I don't get the tools by then, I'm gonna have your ship pick you up again—in a large number of very small boxes. Know what I mean, pal?"

Kalo belatedly began to unload the captured devices onto the Boss's desk. He pointed to a phaser. "This here's a heater, Boss. I don't know what the other junk is."

"A heater, eh? Let's see how it works." He pointed it at a wall. Kirk jerked forward.

"Don't do that! You'll take out half the wall!"

"That good, eh? Great. Just gimme maybe a hundred of these and we don't have no more trouble."

"Out of the question," Kirk said.

"I get what I want." Bela picked up a communicator. "What are these here?"

Kirk remained silent. Jerking a thumb toward McCoy, Bela said to Kalo, "Burn him."

"All right," Kirk said hastily. "It's a communications device, locked onto my ship."

Bela fiddled with one until it snapped open in his hand. "Hey," he said to it. "In the ship."

"Scott here. Who is this?"

"This here's Bela Okmyx. I got your Captain and his

122

friends down here. You want 'em back alive, send me a hundred of them fancy heaters of yours, and some troops to show us how to use them. You got eight hours. Then I put the hit on your friends. Know what I mean?"

"No," Scott's voice said. "But I'll find out."

Bela closed the communicator. "Okay. Kalo, take 'em over to the warehouse. Put 'em in the bag, and keep an eye on 'em, good. You hear?"

"Sure, Boss. Move out, you guys."

The warehouse room had a barred window and was sparsely furnished, but it was equipped with another copy of The Book. Kalo and two henchmen were playing cards at a table, guns handy, their eyes occasionally flicking to Kirk, Spock and McCoy at the other end of the room.

"One book," McCoy said. "And they made it the blueprint for their entire society. Amazing."

"But not unprecedented," Spock said. "At one time, in old Chicago, conventional government nearly broke down. The gangs almost took over."

"This Okmyx must be the worst of the lot."

"Through we may quarrel with his methods, his goal is essentially the correct one," Spock said. "This culture must become united——or it will degenerate into complete anarchy. It is already on the way; you will recall the young women who complained of failing services."

"If this society broke down, because of the influence of the *Horizon,* the Federation is responsible," Kirk said. "We've got to try to straighten the mess out. Spock, if you could get to the sociological banks of the computer, could you come up with a solution?"

"Quite possibly, Captain."

Signaling Spock and McCoy to follow him unobtrusively, Kirk gradually drifted toward the card game. The players looked up at him warily, free hands on guns; but they relaxed again as he pulled over a chair and sat down. The game was a variety of stud poker.

After a few moments, Kirk said, "That's a kid's game."

"Think so?" Kalo said.

"I wouldn't waste my time."

"Who's asking you to?"

"On Beta Antares Four, they play a game for men. Of course, it's probably too involved for you. It takes intelligence."

Antares is not a double star; Kirk had taken the chance in order to warn the sometimes rather literal-minded that he was lying deliberately.

"Okay, I'll bite," Kalo said. "Take the cards, big man. Show us how it's played."

"The Antares cards are different, of course, but not too different," Kirk said, riffling through them. "The game's called Fizzbin. Each player gets six cards—except for the man on the dealer's right, who gets seven. The second card goes up—except on Tuesdays, of course . . . Ah, Kalo, that's good, you've got a nine. That's half a fizzbin already."

"I need another nine?"

Spock and McCoy drew nearer with quite natural curiosity, since neither of them had ever heard of the game. Neither had Kirk.

"Oh, no. That would be a sralk and you'd be disqualified. You need a King or a deuce, except at night, when a Queen or a four would . . . Two sixes! That's excellent—unless, of course, you get another six. Then you'd have to turn it in, unless it was black."

"But if it was black?" Kalo said, hopelessly confused.

"Obviously, the opposite would hold," Kirk said, deciding to throw in a touch of something systematic for further confusion. "Instead of turning your six in, you'd get another card. Now, what you are really hoping for is a royal fizzbin, but the odds against that are, well, astronomical, wouldn't you say, Spock?"

"I have never computed them, Captain."

"Take my word they're considerable. Now the last card around. We call it the cronk, but its home name is *klee-et.** Ready? Here goes."

He dealt, making sure that Kalo's card went off the table. "Oops, sorry."

"I'll get it."

Kalo bent over. In the same instant, Kirk put his hands

---

*A Vulcan word meaning, roughly, "prepare to engage." See "Amok Time," *Star Trek Three*.

under the table and shoved. It went over on the other two. McCoy and Spock were ready; the action was hardly more than a flurry before the three guards were helpless. Kirk parceled out the guns.

"Spock, find the radio transmitting station. Uhura is monitoring their broadcasts. Cut in and have yourself and Bones beamed up to the ship."

"Surely you are coming, Captain?"

"Not without Bela Okmyx."

"Jim, you can't . . ."

"This mess is our responsibility, Bones. You have your orders. Let's go."

Kirk at first felt a little uneasy walking a city street with a submachine gun under his arm, but no one passing seemed to find it unusual. On the contrary, it seemed to be a status symbol; people cleared the way for him.

But the walk ended abruptly with two handguns stuck into his ribs from behind. He had walked into an ambush. How had Bela gotten word so fast?

The answer to that was soon forthcoming. The two hoods who had mousetrapped him crowded him into a car—and the ride was a long one. At its end was another office, almost a duplicate of Bela's; but the man behind the desk was short, squat, bull-shaped and strange. He arose with a jovial smile.

"So you're the Fed. Well, well. I'm Krako—Jojo Krako, Boss of the South Territory. Hey, I'm glad to see you."

"Would you mind telling me how you knew about me?"

"I got all Bela's communications bugged. He can't make a date with a broad without I know about it. Now you're probably wondering why I brought you here."

"Don't tell me. You want to make a deal."

Krako was pleased. "I like that. Sharp. Sharp, huh, boys?"

"Sharp, Boss."

"Let me guess some more," Kirk said. "You want— uh—heaters, right? And troops to teach you how to use them. And you'll hit the other bosses and take over the whole planet. And then we'll sit down and talk, right?"

"Wrong," Krako said. "More than talk. I know Bela.

He didn't offer you beans. Me, I'm a reasonable man. Gimme what I want, and I cut you in for, say, a third. Skimmed right off the top. How do you like that?"

"I've got a better idea. You know this planet has to be united. So let's sit down, you, me, and Bela, get in contact with the other bosses, and discuss the matter like rational men."

Krako seemed to be genuinely outraged. "That ain't by The Book, Kirk. We know how to handle things! You make hits! Somebody argues, you lean on him! You think we're stupid or something?"

"No, Mr. Krako," Kirk said, sighing. "You're not stupid. But you are peculiarly unreasonable."

"Pally, I got ways of getting what I want. You want to live, Kirk? Sure you do. But after I get done with you, you're liable to be sorry—unless you come across. Zabo, tell Cirl the Knife to sharpen up his blade. I might have a job for him." The smile came back. "Of course, you gimme the heaters and you keep your ears."

"No deal."

"Too bad. Put him on ice."

The two hoods led Kirk out.

On shipboard, Spock's fortunes were not running much better. There turned out to be no specifics in the computer, not even a record of a planet-wide culture based on a moral inversion. Without more facts, reason and logic were alike helpless.

"Mr. Spock," Uhura said. "Mr. Okmyx from the surface is making contact. Audio only."

Spock moved quickly to the board. "Mr. Okmyx, this is Spock."

"How'd you get up there?" Bela's voice asked.

"Irrelevant, since we are here."

"Uh—yeah. But you'd better get back down. Krako's put the bag on your Captain."

Spock raised his eyebrows. "Why would he put a bag on the Captain?"

"Kidnapped him, dope. He'll scrag him, too."

"If I understand you correctly, that would seem to be a problem. Have you any suggestions?"

"Sure. You guys got something I want. I can help you get the Captain back. No reason we can't make a deal."

"I am afraid I find it difficult to trust you, sir."

"What's to trust? Business is business. We call a truce. You come down. My boys spring Kirk. Then we talk about you giving me a hand."

"Since we must have our Captain back," Spock said after a moment, "I accept. We shall arrive in your office within ten minutes. Spock out."

McCoy had been standing nearby, listening. "You're going to trust him?"

"If we are to save the Captain, without blatant and forceful interference on the planet, then we must have assistance from someone indigenous. At the moment, we are forced to trust Mr. Okmyx." He turned toward Scott. "Mr. Scott, although I hope to avoid their use, I think you should adjust one of the phaser banks to a strong stun position."

"Now," McCoy said, "you're starting to make sense."

Spock did not reply, since nothing in the situation made sense to him. Trusting Okmyx was nothing short of stupid, and the use of force was forbidden by General Order Number One. In such a case, the only course was to abide by the Captain's principle of letting the situation ripen.

Bela, of course, had a trap arranged. Spock had expected it, but there had been no way to avoid it. What he had not expected—nor had Bela—was the abrupt subsequent appearance of Kirk in the doorway, with a submachine gun under his arm.

"How did you get away?" Spock asked interestedly, after the gangsters had been disarmed—a long process which produced a sizable heap of lethal gadgets, some of them wholly unfamiliar.

"Krako made the mistake of leaving me a radio; that was all I needed for the old trip-wire trick. I thought I told you to get to the ship."

"We have been there, Captain. The situation required our return."

"It may be just as well. Find out anything from the computers?"

"Nothing useful, Captain. Logic and factual knowledge do not seem to apply here."

"You admit that?" McCoy said.

"With the greatest reluctance, Doctor."

"Then you won't mind if I play a hunch?" Kirk said.

"I am not sanguine about hunches, sir, but I have no practical alternative."

"What are you going to do, Jim?"

"Now that I've got Bela," Kirk said, "I'm going to put the bag on Krako."

"On Krako?" Bela said. "You ain't serious?"

"Why not?" Kirk turned to Bela and fingered his suit lapel. "That's nice material."

"It ought to be. It cost a bundle."

"Get out of it. You, too."

"Hey, now, wait a minute . . ."

"Take it off—pally! This time nobody's going to bag me."

Seeing that he meant it, Kalo and Bela got out of their clothes; Kirk and Spock donned them. Scooping up the required submachine guns as passports, they went out, leaving McCoy in charge.

In front of the office sat the large black car that Bela used. Fishing in the pockets of his borrowed suit, Kirk found the keys. They got in.

"Any idea how to run this thing, Spock?"

"No, Captain. But it should not be too difficult."

"Let's see," Kirk said, studying the controls. "A keyhole. For the—ignition process, I think. Insert and turn. Right."

He felt around with his foot and touched a button. The car stuttered and the engine was running.

"Interesting," Spock said.

"As long as it runs. Now, let's see. I think—gears . . ."

He pulled the lever down, which produced nothing but an alarming grinding sound which he could feel in his hand as well as hear.

"As I recall," Spock said, "there was a device called the clutch. Perhaps one of those foot pedals . . ."

The right-hand pedal didn't seem to work, but the left-hand one allowed the gear lever to go down. Kirk let the pedal up cautiously, and the car started with a lurch.

Kirk remembered the way to Krako's offices well enough, but the trip was a wild one; there seemed to be some trick to working the clutch which Kirk hadn't mastered. Luckily, pedestrians gave the big black vehicle a wide berth. Spock just hung on. When it was over, he observed, "Captain, you are a splendid starship commander, but as a taxi driver you leave much to be desired."

"Haven't had time to practice. Leave these clumsy guns under the seat; we'll use phasers."

They made their way to Krako, leaving a trail of stunned guards behind. The Boss did not seem a bit taken aback when they burst in on him; he had four hoods behind him, guns aimed at the door.

"You don't shoot, we don't shoot," he said rapidly.

"This would appear to be an impasse," Spock said.

"Who's your friend with the ears?" Krako asked. "Never mind. Ain't this nice? I was wondering how I was going to get you back, and you delivered yourself! You don't think you'll get out of it this time, do you?"

"We didn't come here for games," Kirk said. "This is bigger than you or Okmyx or any of the others."

The phaser which Krako had previously taken from Kirk was on the desk, still on safety lock. Krako nudged it. "Don't talk fancy. All you gotta do is tell me how to work these things."

"Krako," Kirk said, "can you trust all your men?"

"Yeah, sure. I either trust 'em or they're dead."

"Maybe. But when it comes to weapons like these— well, one of them could make a man a pretty big boss around here."

Krako thought about it. At last he said, "Zabo and Karf, stay put. You other guys vanish . . . All right, these two is okay. Now that we got no busy little eyes around, how do you work this thing?"

Kirk moved in on Krako hard and fast, spitting his words out like bullets. "Knock it off, Krako. We don't have time to show you how to play with toys."

"Toys?"

"What do you think we're here for, Krako? To get a

cut of your deal? Forget it. That's peanuts to an outfit like the Federation."

"It is?" Krako said, a little dazed by the sudden switch.

"Unquestionably," Spock said.

"We came here to take over, Krako. The whole ball of wax. Maybe, if you cooperate, we'll cut *you* in for a piece of the action."

"A minute piece," Spock added.

"How much is that?" Krako asked.

"We'll figure it out later."

"But—I thought you guys had some kind of law about no interference . . ."

"Who'd interfering? We're just taking over."

Spock seemed slightly alarmed. "Uh—Captain . . ."

"Cool it, Spocko. Later."

"What's your deal?" Krako asked.

Kirk motioned him to his feet and, when the bewildered gangster stood, Kirk sat down in his chair and swung his feet up onto the desk. He appropriated one of Krako's cigars.

"The Federation wants this planet, but we don't want to have to come in and use our muscle. That ain't subtle. So what we do is help one guy take over. He pulls the planet's strings—and we pull his. Follow?"

"But what's your cut?"

Kirk eyed the unlit cigar judiciously. "What do you care, so long as you're in charge? Right, Spocko?"

"Right on the button, Boss," Spock said, falling into his role a little belatedly but with a certain relish. "Of course, there's always Bela Okmyx . . ."

Krako thought only a moment. "You got a deal. Call your ship and bring down your boys and whatever you need."

Kirk got to his feet and snapped open his communicator. "Kirk to *Enterprise*."

*"Enterprise.* Scott here, sir."

"Scotty, we made the deal with Krako."

"Uh—we did, sir?"

"We're ready to make the hit. We're taking over the whole planet as soon as you can get ready."

"Is that wise, sir?"

"Sure, we can trust Krako—he doesn't have any choice. He's standing here right now, *about three feet to my left,* all ready to be our pal. I'd like to show him the ship, just so he's sure I'm giving him the straight dope. But you know how it is."

"Oh aye, sir," Scott said. "I know indeed."

"We'll be needing enough phasers to equip all of Krako's men, plus advisers—troops to back them up on the hit. You moving, Scotty?"

"Aye, Uhura's on to the Transporter Room and two of the boys are on their way. Ready when you say the word."

"Very well, Scotty, begin."

Krako looked curiously at Kirk. "You mean you're gonna start bringing all those guys down now?"

"No—not exactly." As he spoke, the hum of the Transporter effect filled the room, and Krako shimmered out of existence. Zabo and Karf stared, stunned—and a second later were stunned more thoroughly.

"Well played—Spocko."

Spock winced. "So we have—put the bag on Krako. What is our next maneuver, Captain?"

"Back to Bela's place."

"In the car, Captain?"

"It's faster than walking. Don't tell me you're afraid of cars, Spock."

"Not at all. It is your driving which alarms me."

Through the door of Bela's office, they heard McCoy saying worriedly, "Where *are* they?"

And then Bela's, "Knowing Krako, we'll be lucky if he sends 'em back on a blotter."

Kirk walked in. "Wrong again, Okmyx." He brushed past the relieved McCoy. "Outta my way, Sawbones. I want to talk to this guy. I'm getting tired of playing patty-cake with you penny ante operators."

"Who you calling penny ante?" Bela said, bristling.

"Nobody but you, baby. Now listen. The Federation's moving in here. We're taking over, and if you play ball, we'll leave a piece of the pie for you. If you don't, you're out. All the way out. Got that?" He shoved the phaser under Bela's nose to make the point.

"Yeah—yeah, sure, Kirk. Why didn't you say so in the first place? I mean—all you hadda do was explain."

The communicator came out. "Scotty, you got Krako on ice up there?"

"Aye, Captain."

"Keep him till I ask for him. We're going to be making some old-style phone calls from these coordinates. Lock on at the receiving end and transport the party here to us. Okay, Okmyx. Start calling the other bosses."

Shrugging, Bela went to the phone and dialed four times. "Hello, Tepo? Guess who? . . . Yeah, I got a lot of nerve. What're you going to do about it?"

With a hum, Tepo materialized, holding a non-existent phone in his hand. McCoy moved in to disarm him.

". . . coming over there with a couple of my boys, and . . . Brother!"

Bela grinned at Kirk. "Hey, this ain't bad."

"Keep dialing."

Half an hour later, the office was crowded with dazed gang leaders, Krako among them. Kirk climbed up on the desk, now cradling a local gun to add weight to his argument.

"All right, pipe down, everybody. I'll tell you what you're going to do. The Federation just took over around here, whether you like it or not. You guys have been running this planet like a piecework factory. From here on, it's all under one roof. You're going to form a syndicate and run this planet like a business. That means you make a profit."

"Yeah?" Tepo called. "And what's your percentage?"

"I'm cutting the Federation in for forty per cent." He leveled the gun. "You got objections?"

Tepo had obviously had guns pointed at him too many times to be cowed. "Yeah. I hear a lot of talk, but all I see here is you and a couple of your boys. I don't see no Federation."

"Listen, they got a ship," Krako said. "I know—I been there."

"Yeah, but Tepo's got a point," Bela said. "All we ever see is them."

"I only saw three other guys and a broad while I was in the ship," Krako said. "Maybe there ain't any more?"

"There are four hundred . . ."

Kirk was interrupted by an explosion outside, followed by a fusillade of shots. Krako, who was nearest the window, peered around the edge of it.

"It's my boys," he reported. "Must think I'm still in the ship. They're making a hit on this place."

"My boys'll put 'em down," Bela said.

"Wanna bet?"

Kirk's communicator was already out. "Scotty, put ship's phasers on stun and fire a burst in a one-block radius around these coordinates, excluding this building."

"Right away, sir."

Kirk looked at the confused gangsters. "Gentlemen, you are about to see the Federation at work."

The noise roared on a moment more, and then the window was lit up with the phaser effect. Dead silence fell promptly.

Krako smiled weakly and swallowed. "Some trick."

"They're not dead, just knocked out for a while," Kirk said. "We could just as easily have killed them."

"Okay," Bela said. "We get the message. You were saying something about a syndicate."

"No, he was saying something about a percentage," Tepo said. "You sure forty percent is enough?"

"I think it will be just fine. We'll send someone around to collect it every year—and give you advice if you need it."

"That's reasonable," Bela said. He glared at the others. "Ain't that reasonable?"

There was a murmur of assent. Kirk smiled cheerfully. "Well, in that case, pull out some of that drinking stuff of yours, Okmyx, and let's get down to the talking."

The bridge of the *Enterprise* was routinely busy. Kirk was in the command chair, feeling considerably better to be back in uniform.

"I must say," Spock said, "your solution to the problem on Iotia is unconventional, Captain. But it does seem to be the only workable one."

"What troubles you is that it isn't logical to leave a criminal organization in charge. Is that it?"

"I do have some reservations. And how do you propose to explain to Starfleet Command that a starship will be sent around each year to collect 'our cut,' as you put it?"

" 'Our cut' will be put back into the planet's treasury—and the advisers and collectors can help steer the Iotians back into a more conventional moral and ethical system. In the meantime, the syndicate forms a central government that can effectively administer to the needs of the people. That's a step in the right direction. Our group of 'governors' is already learning to take on conventional responsibilities. Guiding them is—our piece of the action."

Spock pondered. "Yes, it seems to make sense. Tell me, Captain. Whatever gave you so outlandish an idea—and where did you pick up all that jargon so quickly?"

Kirk grinned. "Courtesy of Krako. A radio wasn't all he left in my cell. He also left me some reading matter."

"Ah, of course. The Book."

"Spocko, now you're talkin'."